The crackle of rifles was suddenly all around Charley as he beat his drum with fingers slick with sweat. To his right he saw Jem Miller, his legs pumping toward the Confederates' logs. The boy looked on in horror as Jem dropped his musket, spread wide his arms, and crumpled onto the ground. Jem dead? Dead in the early afternoon light of such a warm spring day? It could not be. In Charley's brain something howled, "No!"

Charley ran to his fallen friend. In a flash, he had Jem's musket to his shoulder. Taking aim, little Charley Quinn chose his man, a lanky, brown-bearded Confederate standing atop the logs. Charley fired. The Rebel dropped his gun and clutched at his shoulder. Blood began to well between his fingers, and he fell backward.

Now the truth flooded Charley's consciousness. He was only twelve years old, and he'd shot and killed a human being.

Praise for <u>Charley Skedaddle</u>

"Beatty brings history to life with . . . unusual characters and events, and fascinating historic detail."

—*School Library Journal*

"The settings . . . are quite powerful. These, along with Charley's disillusionment and change . . . make [this novel] one of Beatty's best."

—*Publishers Weekly*

"What gives this book its shimmer and forward thrust is the rich detail of each aspect of Charley's journey. Young readers . . . will love the rousing epic."

—*Kirkus Reviews*, pointer

"Beatty writes with the practiced hand of a good storyteller, and her underlying themes of bravery and self-esteem are as much a concern today as one-hundred-odd years ago."

—*Booklist*

CHARLEY SKEDADDLE

PATRICIA BEATTY

Troll

In the hope that his generation
will never have to go to war,
I dedicate this book to my grandson,
Seth Aaron Weiner.

CONTENTS

1 A BOWERY BOY

As he set the hatbox on a crate beside him, Charley Quinn heard the words in his head: "If ever you got to fight alone, Charley, me lad, get your back to a wall!"

Right now it was as if his older brother, Johnny, had spoken to him. His words flashed through Charley's mind as the thickset boy, a member of the Dead Rabbits gang, walked menacingly toward him through the cool March rain of early dusk.

Carefully, twelve-year-old Charley stepped backward to the brick wall, his feet planted firmly in the mud of the Bowery alley, his fists raised and ready the way Johnny had taught him. This was how the best, most famous boxers in New York City fought. Johnny had known all about them. He'd even met a few in saloons. Before he'd gone off to war at twenty-three, he'd been the best street fighter in the Bowery and chief of the Bowery Boys gang.

Charley's eyes bored into the dimness of the dirty alley, looking for help from one of the other Bowery Boys. There was no chance of aid from his brother. Johnny

Quinn, who had fought bravely against the Dead Rabbits in the great fight of 1857, handsome Johnny, lay now under the earth in Pennsylvania at a place called Gettysburg. Gone off to be a soldier, he'd died last year, falling with the other heroes of the 140th New York Veterans Volunteers.

Charley knew, too, that there'd be no help from the other members of his gang. He'd left them ten minutes ago at one of the new shooting galleries the Bowery boasted. Why hadn't he stayed longer with them and let his sister wait a bit more? Now he'd been caught by a prowling Dead Rabbit, alone and weary from hours of dodging the dangerous horse-drawn omnibuses on Broadway. This would be a one-on-one fight, because no other members of the Dead Rabbits gang were around, either. Well, that was good. He had no fear of a one-on-one fight.

The Dead Rabbit spoke first, raising his voice over the roar of busy Broadway, a few streets away. "A Bowery Boy, ain'tcha? You wouldn't be here if you wasn't."

"You bet," cried Charley. "And I can tell from the red stripes on your britches that you're a Dead Rabbit. What're you doing here?"

"I'm passin' through. I'd be Tom Bailey from Mott Street. You want to fight?"

Charley replied, "Are you planning to fight me with a knife? If you are, I tell you I got one, too, and it's sharp enough to suit me."

The Dead Rabbit scoffed. "My fists'll do tonight. That'll be plenty for the likes of you no-good Irisher."

"Come and try this Irisher," was Charley's taunt.

"Come and try me, Tom Bailey."

The Dead Rabbit took the challenge. Running forward, he flung himself at Charley, his fists flailing wildly.

Coolly, as Johnny had taught him, Charley ducked the first punches, catching those meant for his face on his forearms and swinging shoulders. Then when Tom, in his rush, had gone too far off-balance, Charley came in under his guard with a hard left to the side of his head, followed by a harder right to his nose.

Howling, Tom fell back holding his nose, now streaming blood.

The Dead Rabbit wasn't through, though. He came charging back at Charley, fighting more warily now. One of his punches landed on Charley's left eye and another on his cheek. Charley groaned—not from the pain he felt but for what Noreen Quinn and Mr. Demarest would say when they saw his bruised face. He'd hoped to win this fight unmarked.

Angry now, Charley sailed into the Dead Rabbit, punching hard and kicking, too, because when the two gangs clashed, they didn't fight by any rules. One of Charley's feet shot out behind Tom's left one and hooked it. Surging backward, he brought the Dead Rabbit down and leapt on him as he lay on his back in a large, shallow mud puddle. Straddling Tom Bailey, aware that he was getting the knees of his best trousers wet and muddy, Charley gestured with his fist and asked, "Have you had enough of me for now?"

"Yeah, yeah. I've had enough."

Just then a loud, deep, masculine voice called out, "I

3

think ye've both had enough!" and Charley felt a strong hand pluck him off the Dead Rabbit and set him onto his feet. "Ye, ye run," the man ordered Tom, "and don't let me see ye here again, ye hear!"

Tom got up swiftly, his nose still bleeding. He glared at Charley and the huge policeman and fled down the alley.

"Let me go!" squawked Charley as the big Irishman in the long blue coat and gold-painted helmet held him up, his feet swinging.

The Metropolitan only laughed. Suddenly he let the boy fall to a crouch in the mire. He said, "Ah, I've seen ye before. Ye were with Noreen Quinn. Ye have the look of each other, the Quinn look, the red hair, the pale face, and the eyes of blue."

Panting, Charley nodded. "Yes, I'd be her brother."

"And fightin', too. That was a Dead Rabbit ran away just now, so ye'd be a Bowery Boy."

It was wisest not to admit the truth, so Charley muttered, "I don't belong to any gang."

"A likely story. I know ye to be a Bowery Boy, all right, the youngest one of all, even if ye aren't wearin' yer red shirt now. I knew yer brother, Johnny Quinn, before he went off to war and got hisself killed at Round Top. If he hadn't enlisted, he might've died in another scrap like the one in '57 between yer gang and the Rabbits. I saw it. It lasted long enough fer the state militia to be called out to stop it. Hundreds of ye was there."

Wiping mud and rain from his face, Charley said nothing. The important thing now was to get away from this Metropolitan. The man knew too much about him.

It was on the tip of his tongue to tell him that his brother never would have been killed in a street fight in New York. He'd been too smart for that. But instead Charley said, "You didn't arrest that Dead Rabbit, so you shouldn't take me in, either."

"I don't intend to."

Charley breathed deep with relief. He turned to pick up the hatbox and leave, but once more that hand reached out to collar him. The Metropolitan said, "I don't intend to arrest ye, but I do intend to take ye home to yer sister."

"I was going there, anyway. How do you know my sister?" demanded Charley.

"I seen her and her young feller Michael Demarest at Mass on Sundays. I seen ye with her there—one time only it was. From walkin' my beat I know she lives on Chrystie Street."

Wanting to be rid of the policeman as soon as possible, Charley started to move off when the big hand stopped him once more. "Jest one thing more, young Quinn. Did ye thieve that box ye have with ye?"

Stung, the boy told him, "No, I didn't! It's my sister's. I work with her. I take the bonnets she trims to Genin's on Broadway and fetch back the untrimmed ones and ribbons and laces she needs from R. H. Macy's and Lord and Taylor's. Look in the box if you don't believe me! There's nothing there but bonnets."

The Metropolitan laughed. "I believe ye. I was but teasin'. I spotted ye afar with the hatbox. Quite the little gent ye looked, if I didn't know better about ye. I plan to deliver ye home before there's another Dead Rabbit after

5

ye. Come along with me now."

Held fast by the collar, Charley and the policeman paraded through the gaslit Bowery, past concert saloons, oyster houses, leather-goods stores, grogshops, and dance halls filled with loud music and shrill laughter. The laughter from the many billiard parlors was deeper because women didn't go into them. The sharp crack-crack of rifles struck his ears from the shooting galleries. Inside one he spied members of his gang, but their backs were turned to him as they waited for their chance with the rifles. Johnny had been a fine shot at the shooting galleries, and Charley himself was doing better all the time. It wasn't fair that a Rebel bullet had gotten his brother at Gettysburg before he'd fired off one shot himself. That one bullet had killed him.

One shout of help from him, Charley knew, would bring some of his gang tumbling out to argue with the Metropolitan, but he didn't cry out to them. He was too embarrassed. How they'd laugh to see him almost dangling at the end of the policeman's arm, tripping along like a lady toe dancer. He knew he looked ridiculous. Whiskery men in top hats and long black cloaks and women in bright-colored hoopskirt gowns laughed as they passed him. Soldiers in Union blue went by laughing, too, while the hooves of horses drawing streetcars on rails and noisy, iron-rimmed carriage wheels splashed more mud on him and his captor.

The Metropolitan propelled Charley into the entryway of a two-story brown-brick building and up two flights of steps. He stopped at the door where the Quinns lived in three small, shabbily furnished rooms and rapped.

To Charley's dismay it wasn't Noreen who opened the door but the man she was pledged to marry: tall, lean, black-haired Michael Demarest. Behind him, Charley could see his sister and another seamstress, her friend Mrs. O'Neill. Noreen rose from her sewing machine, looking alarmed.

The hateful Mr. Demarest, in the cold way he had about him, asked, "Ah, Sergeant, what have you brought to my door?"

His door? Anger grew high in Charley Quinn. This little dingy flat had been rented by his parents long ago when they first came from Ireland. His father had gone west to work on the canals when Charley had been a baby and had never been heard of again. His mother had died of consumption five years back. But the Quinns had stayed on in the flat. Noreen, the oldest of them all at twenty-seven, had paid the rent and bought most of the food with the money she earned from her skills with the needle. No one trimmed hats better or faster in the city. First Johnny, then Charley, had delivered bonnets for her.

The policeman said with a deep, rumbling chuckle, "I'd say in truth 'tis a drowned rat I have here. Might as well take him, anyway!"

The hatbox fell from his hand and skidded across the floor as Charley was pushed onto the floor to fall at his sister's feet. When he looked up into her black-fringed blue eyes, he saw pain and embarrassment there, and sad weariness, too.

She told the officer, "Thank ye, sir, for fetchin' him home to me. I see he's been fightin'. Is he hurt bad?"

"No, I'm not," growled Charley. "It was just fists."

Michael Demarest mocked, "What, no pistols or clubs or knives this time? How many of you were there? A hundred, at least, I suppose."

Charley flared, "Just me and the Rabbit. I wish it'd been more."

He looked at the man with hatred. A clerk in a bank, that was all Demarest was, a pen-pusher. He hadn't gone into the Army when Johnny had, though his brother had expected him to. Demarest had weak eyes. Weak indeed? His glasses were thick but not so thick that he hadn't spotted pretty Noreen Quinn at Mass two years ago and made her acquaintance with boldness. Demarest loved money, and Noreen made decent wages—more than she could have made working as a housemaid in a big house on Fifth Avenue where rich people lived. She took work into her own home, toiling far into the night at her sewing machine. The whir of its treadle had been a lullaby to Charley when he was very small.

How could she marry this stingy stick of a man who considered a stroll in new and handsome Central Park or a ride on a horse-drawn omnibus a great treat to Noreen from him? If Johnny were alive, he'd put a stop to that. Noreen and Demarest had only been betrothed for six months.

While Charley glared, the Metropolitan told Noreen, "The other lad was gettin' the worst of it. 'Tis only fair to say so."

Charley got up and said to the policeman, "I thank you for telling her I was winning." He stood watching as the man touched his fingers to his helmet brim to Noreen and a silent Mrs. O'Neill and closed the door behind him.

In an instant Noreen was on to Charley. In a fury, she cried, "Fightin' again, are ye? Ye promised me, Charley Quinn, that ye'd fight no more while ye did errands for me. Look at ye. Those are yer best clothes."

Charley wiped his face with the torn sleeve of his black-and-white checked suit. He looked down at his high-buttoned boots, more brown now than black with alley mud, and at his filthy stockings and stained knee pants. He'd looked a jim-dandy delivering bonnets to the milliners that day. He'd been smiling and soft-spoken and polite wherever he'd gone. Not only was it Noreen's money and the change from her purchases that jingled in his pockets, but also tips from the ladies he'd charmed. All had gone right as could be until he'd met the Dead Rabbit. That was bad luck of the worst sort.

Noreen demanded, "Why did ye fight in yer best clothes? Why do ye fight at all?"

"I had to fight tonight. He came at me first. He was a Dead Rabbit. I couldn't run away from him, could I?"

"And why not?"

Charley looked in despair at Demarest, who, he thought, ought to understand at least this much about manliness. But the man only smiled his thin smile without nodding. What kind of Irishman was he?

"Why not *run*?" Charley protested to his sister. "If I ran, my gang would be sure to hear about it."

"And what is so wrong about that? Michael and I are gettin' married next month. We just decided. Then we'll all of us move across town to a nicer place. That will be the end of yer Bowery Boys and yer Dead Rabbits, too. I hate them all. Mother hated it when Johnny was a Bowery Boy and now ye are, too."

"I have to be one, Noreen—because of him."

"No, ye don't have to be! Now go wash yer face. I say ye are to stay in tonight. We were only waitin' for ye to come home so we can go out to Niblo's Theater. Mrs. O'Neill is treatin' us. Her husband sent money to her from the Army. If ye hadn't ruined yer suit, ye could go, too."

"Yes, Charley, ye were invited, too," said Mrs. O'Neill, a plump, black-haired woman older than Noreen.

Charley mumbled, "I don't want to go to Niblo's." Now, for the first time, he noticed that his sister was wearing her dark blue taffeta gown with the white rosebuds at the neck. She always looked like a grand lady in it.

Walking stiff-legged past Demarest, Charley went to the tiny room he had shared with Johnny. He turned up the gas lamp, lit it, and then picked up the full water pitcher. Pouring its contents into the basin, he got his towel from the washstand and looked into his piece of broken mirror. He saw with fierce joy that his eye was already turning black and his cheek was red and torn. It had been a good fight even if it had come at the wrong time.

Dabbing at his face with the wet towel, he heard Demarest's voice through his partially open door. "I tell you, Noreen, that brother of yours ought to be kept in a cage. I'll put up with him living with us if you insist, though you know I don't fancy him or want him. If he comes with us, I'll see that your Charley toes my mark."

Noreen's voice was wheedling. "And if he doesn't, Michael? He's a lot like Johnny. Nobody could ever do a thing with him."

"Then, my dear, your brother will go to a home for incorrigible boys or to an orphanage. Nothing must come between us and our love, nothing and no one. There are places for boys like Charley."

Charley held his breath. What would his sister say? Would she order Demarest out right now?

Just then Mrs. O'Neill put in, "Michael has the right of it, Noreen."

Again there was silence, then Noreen Quinn said softly, "Yes, Michael, Charley must behave better. He'll understand when I tell him. I'll speak with him in the morning and he'll behave. . . ."

Unwilling to hear more, Charley plunged his whole head into the basin, sputtering like the ocean seal he'd seen in a tank at P. T. Barnum's Museum. He felt sick to his stomach. Noreen would tell him tomorrow, would she? She'd let him squirm under the thumb of Mr. Michael Demarest? She'd take him away from the Bowery Boys, Johnny's gang, his only friends? Didn't she know how much he missed Johnny, the volunteer fireman, strongest man on the pumps in the Tompkins No. 30 Engine Company on Chrystie Street?

Lifting his dripping head, Charley heard the door closing into the hallway. Anger rose inside him. The devil Noreen would take him away from the Bowery! The devil Demarest would keep him a prisoner even if he wanted to drag him all the way out to Harlem to live on a little farm! Be damned if he'd stay inside tonight!

2 THE MEN IN BLUE

Twenty minutes later, dressed in the plug hat, black jacket, red flannel shirt, high-heeled boots, and broadcloth trousers that were the uniform of the Bowery Boys, Charley hurried down the wet, gaslit street to find his gang. Would they still be at the shooting galleries? Probably not. Bowery Boys never stayed long in one place. There was always plenty to do in the Bowery.

Charley walked boldly, not afraid of any Metropolitans he might meet. The clothes he wore and the knife in his pocket gave him courage. He'd have preferred to carry Johnny's fancy knife with the staghorn handle, but that had gone to Gettysburg with him and not come home to him and Noreen. His silver watch had, though, and Charley always had it with him.

The Bowery Boys were not at the shooting galleries, and no one he asked seemed to know where they had gone. His head high, proud of the black eye and torn cheek that showed he had not run away from a scrap, Charley moved jauntily as a Bowery Boy should, darting in and out of the loud and flashily dressed city crowds that came to this part of New York for a good time. This is where he belonged. This was his part of the city. Sitting in the flat with Noreen, he sometimes felt he couldn't get his breath, but here in the Bowery he could.

He had fifty cents in his pocket. Where should he go? He wished it was already April and the Metropolitan Fair had opened. It would do the city proud. Noreen had read about the exhibits to him from *The Times*. He wanted to see the Indian tents and the captured battle flags from the Mexican War and the "hairy eagle" that the governor of Illinois's wife had made from the hair of the heads of President Lincoln and his cabinet officers and senators. By April, he hoped to have a whole extra silver dollar to put into the box that would be under the eagle. The money was to be used for the Sanitary Commission that ran Army hospitals to help Union soldiers wounded in battles. If he gave a dollar, he would also be able to sign the album that would be going to Abe Lincoln along with the hairy eagle after the fair closed. Abe could read his name, "Charles Stephen Quinn," along with all the other signers. Oh, he could hardly wait for the fair. He'd be there the first day, for sure.

But that was for April. What should he do right now? Should he go to Barnum's Museum to look at the giants and the tiny people, like General Tom Thumb and his even tinier wife? Should he see the huge snake Barnum had there or the creature that was called the "What is it?" Wherever he decided to go, it wouldn't be to Niblo's Theater where his sister and Mr. Demarest were.

Standing in front of a cloak shop in Chatham Square,

Charley turned up his coat collar against the now heavy rain and scanned the street for Bowery Boys and Dead Rabbits. No one was about in this downpour.

As a tall, black carriage came down the street, slowing when it neared him, Charley fastened his gaze on it. It was a fine carriage drawn by a dapple-gray horse and driven by a coachman in a high silk hat and dark green coat. A gentleman's carriage, for sure!

Running from his shelter, Charley kept pace with the carriage along the street. When it stopped in front of a restaurant, Charley dashed forward to pull down the carriage's folded stop for the passengers to step down on. Sometimes swells, fancy gents, paid a whole ten cents to a boy who did that.

A gent in a beaver hat and a black coat came down first. He looked at Charley, fumbled in his watch pocket, and brought out a coin, which he tossed to him. Charley caught it in the air and then took down the rain-wet step. After he stepped down, the man lifted out a giggling girl in a black velvet cloak that covered a magenta satin skirt. In her yellow hair was a wreath of red roses and green ivy leaves. As she passed, Charley sniffed her sweet, flowery perfume. Her escort led her to the walk and, with his gold-topped cane, pushed away a drunken man who had lurched into them, then went on cursing.

Charley grinned as he looked at the two of them. Ten cents, as he had hoped. He moved back into the entrance of a saloon listening to the high, reedy voice of a woman singing "Fairest Rose of Summer." He could scarcely hear her over the din of splashing water, horses' hooves, screeching carriage wheels, and the shouts of drunken men. Oh, it was bound to be a fine Saturday night, and he could make money if he stayed right here and waited for his gang. There would be other carriages and more rich men with pretty ladies who laughed a lot at everything their escorts said. Some Bowery dance halls had new orchestras, and some saloons now had singers and dancers who would attract plenty of pleasure seekers. Charley knew all about the new attractions. He had seen some of them himself and had read about others in *The New York Times*.

Suddenly Charley heard music, not the fiddle-and-pianoforte kind that came from the dance houses but the bright sound of a brass band. A night parade! Maybe a military parade? New York had them all the time these days, and Charley loved them.

He looked up and down the street and saw nothing, so he hurried toward Broadway, pushing past drunken men going in and out of saloons. Yes, there it was. Stepping lively were lines of musket-carrying, marching men led by a brass band. Out of respect, carriages and carts moved to the curbs and streetcars stopped to permit passage over their rails. Yankee soldiers! Men in the Union blue with haversacks, knapsacks, and bedrolls, going off to fight for Abe Lincoln against slavery. By Jiminy, weren't they grand and glorious, though? Charley caught his breath, thrilled to see the green silken flag borne by the color-bearer. The 140th New York Volunteers, Johnny's regiment!

Tears stung Charley's eyes. He was wiping them away when he heard his name called out in a high voice. "Hey, Charley Quinn! Hey, Charley!"

He had heard that voice somewhere before. Was it a Bowery Boy? No. Charley looked swiftly around him but saw none of his gang. Did it come from the other watchers then? No.

There it was again. "Hey, Charley Quinn!" It came from the marching soldiers.

Charley's eyes swept their ranks. After a moment, he spotted the man who had hailed him. He was a tall lamppost of a soldier with lank, fair hair. Could it be? Yes, it was. Con! Con Sullivan. He had been one of Johnny's newly made friends and had brought the bad news of Johnny's death along with the silver watch back to him and Noreen after the battle of Gettysburg. Because he'd been wounded there, Con had left the Army and gone back to work on Long Island, his home. He'd never been a Bowery Boy, but then you had to live in the Bowery to be that lucky.

"Con, hey, Con!" Leaping from where he stood, Charley splashed down to the marchers, waving his hat. Half running beside the soldiers to keep up with their pace, Charley called out, "Why're you back in the Army, Con?"

"To see the end of the scrappin'! We've got the old Johnny Rebs on the run," shouted the man. "When Abe Lincoln put out a call for more men, I came back to my old regiment. I'm well enough now to fight some more. I hoped to see ye and say hello as I went by." The man reached out a long arm, pulled Charley to his side, and half carried him along. The pungent, sour smell of whiskey clung to the Irishman, but Charley didn't care. Living in the Bowery, you soon got used to this odor, and

Johnny had lifted a glass or two with his friends many a time. So what if Con was a little drunk now?

"I see ye been fightin'," Con observed. "Think you're old enough to shoulder a musket, Charley, my lad?"

How like his brother Con Sullivan was. He made Charley feel nine feet tall walking along beside him.

Charley boasted, "I won the fight. I'm a Bowery Boy now, like Johnny was. Sure I can carry a musket. I go to shooting galleries the way he used to. I shoot good. I can hit things a lot smaller'n a Johnny Reb. Where's the 140th going now, Con?"

"I dunno. We're reinforcements right now, and we're all goin' to wherever the rest of the old regiment is. We're headed to the ships." Con let go of Charley's arm, but the boy grabbed it again, hung on, and was dragged along.

"Oh, Con, take me with you! Noreen's getting hitched up with somebody I don't like. They're going to leave the Bowery for someplace else and"—Charley took a deep breath—"throw me in an orphan's home." Well, it hadn't been too much of a lie.

Con's mouth opened in amazement as Charley tightened his grip on him. "What a thing to do! Such sisterly wickedness!"

Glancing away from Con, Charley spied some of his Bowery Boys a distance ahead of the marchers up the street. They would see him marching along with the men in blue. He knew they'd be impressed that a soldier seemed so fond of him. Most of them vowed that as soon as they were old enough, they'd enlist like Johnny Quinn had.

"Take me along with you, Con, *please!*"

For a moment the man's face twisted with thought, then he boomed, "Sure, Charley. Why not? I got five days' cooked rations with me. Ye can share 'em."

A short man with brown sideburns and a dark face in the ranks next to Con said, "He's only a shirttail kid, Con."

"No matter, Jem Miller. The Army's got uses for kids. Ye keep up with us men, Charley, ye hear. Ye let go of me now."

"I'll keep up, you bet." As Charley trotted past the Bowery Boys, he waved his hat and shouted, "I'm off to join the Army!"

At first they looked surprised, and then he heard their cheering, and that warmed his heart. It was the only cheering that was going on. Except for youths like Charley, New York City was weary of the war after two long years of it, weary of the hated draft, of the violent riots protesting it.

After what seemed like a very long march to short-legged Charley Quinn, the troops arrived at the Battery and turned onto a street that brought them to a dock and a waiting ocean steamer.

Here on the wharf, the soldiers broke ranks and waited until told to form pairs to board. Con hurriedly slipped off his equipment, greatcoat, and the blue jacket beneath it. Flinging his open jacket over Charley, he told him, "Hunker down so ye won't be spotted." Turning to a grinning, heavyset soldier near him, he then said, "Put yer coat over the lad, too, so's we hide him."

"Sure, Sullivan."

Crouching down between the two soldiers, Charley marched down the dock, over the gangplank, and onto the deck with no officer spying him.

From the deck of the steamer, the three of them went down narrow steps to between decks. The visibility here was very poor, and the seaweed-scented air was difficult to breathe. Three hatches were open above the men to let in the night air. Peering through the lantern-lit gloom, Charley noticed that there were no chairs or benches or bunks down here.

At once, Con's whiskey bottle came out of his pocket and he took a long swallow, crying, "Here's to new glory for the 140th New York and the little recruit we just got for it! Here's to the memory of young Colonel Pat O'Rourke and Johnny Quinn, who fell at Gettysburg! The boy ye see with me is Johnny's brother. Travelin' with us won't cost him a red cent. We're all the guests of Abe Lincoln, and here's to him, too!" And Con took a second swallow.

As the rest of the marchers came down, Charley Quinn seated himself on the wooden deck next to Con. He promised himself he would write to Noreen and tell her everything once he'd got to wherever he was going with Johnny's old regiment. She'd have a load off her hands with him gone. Even though he'd helped her out plenty, now that she was marrying Demarest, she didn't need him anymore.

Now the boy noticed that the soldier who had said Charley was only a shirttail kid sat on the deck across from him. He was the sour one Con had called Jem. Jem shook his head at Charley and looked down at his heavy shoes as if his feet hurt from marching.

As he peered around him, Charley's heart grew lighter. This was a real ship! He'd never been on a big oceangoing vessel before. Born on Manhattan Island, he'd never left it except for a picnic ferryboat excursion on a paddle-wheel steamer that he, some of his classmates, and a few priests from his school had gone on three years ago. All he had ever known was New York City—the coal smoke and horsy smell that hung in its air, the many noises of its traffic and thousands of people. He knew the shops and, above all, the lively, delightfully wicked Bowery. And where was he going now?

Con Sullivan nudged him, gave him a wink, then said, "Not to worry, Charley. Ye're with me. I won't let no Johnny Reb get ye!"

A Confederate? A Johnny Reb? Charley nodded. It was one of those gray-coated devils who had marched up to Pennsylvania from the South and killed his brother. Charley nodded again. He had a score to settle with the Rebs, a personal one. He told Sullivan proudly, "You won't have to protect me from any Rebels."

The man reached out and gave Charley a gentle punch on the shoulder. "A fire-eater, ain'tcha? I been so busy trainin' these men on Hart Island that I never once seen a newspaper from New York City. How's the talk goin' about diggin' them tunnels for a railroad so's there won't be so much crowdin' on the street? Do ye think they'll dig 'em, Charley?"

The boy shrugged. He'd been hearing about that idea all year. He said, "Maybe the streets on top of 'em would fall in. I wouldn't want to be on Broadway if that happens." He changed the subject. "I bet we're going way down South on this ship."

"Maybe so," Con answered noncommittally.

Soon the between-decks area was crowded with soldiers, all of whom seemed to bring out pipes and cigars and light them. The air had been bad enough, but soon it grew so thick that it was hard to see anyone distinctly unless he was close.

More hidden whiskey came out now from deep pockets. Men grew drunk enough to dance, sing—and to fight one another. Charley moved closer to Con, who was half asleep by now because he'd had so much whiskey. Guards came down between decks to break up the fights. They beat the fighting men with clubbed rifles, then drove them up the gangway.

Jem came over to Charley. He grabbed him by the collar and dragged him away from Con to the very end of the deck, where the two of them sat together with their backs to a bulkhead. From there Charley watched drunken soldiers try to climb up the gangway to the upper deck or crawl up through the open hatches. But they were all shoved back by watchful guards, who stepped on their hands. It was worse than anything Charley had ever seen in the Bowery.

Jem spoke to him in a low growl. "Scum of the earth, some of 'em are. Most of 'em only joined up for the bounty money. Your friend Con got a chunk of cash. That's why he joined up."

Astonished, Charley asked, "Not to fight and see the end of the war?"

Jem laughed for the first time. "No, it was for the

money. He's no better and no worse than hundreds of others here."

"But he didn't tell me the truth!"

Again Jem laughed. "Stay here with me, son. The wild brutes'll fall to sleep soon with all the whiskey they been swilling. They'll be too sick tomorrow to fight. They'll be safer to be around then."

Charley asked, "Why is it you don't fight?"

"I fight, but I don't drink. I got wounded at Fredericksburg last year. I only joined again to help end this war. It's time for it to end. I'm a printer by trade. I was in another regiment at Fredericksburg. It doesn't matter to me where I fight—so long as I fight the Rebels and get this over with. I got no bounty money. I volunteered."

Charley nodded with pride. "So did my brother, Johnny. He got killed at Gettysburg at Round Top."

"Those were different days," said Jem as he stood up to shove away a lurching drunk intent on hitting him and starting a fight.

Late that night, the steamer left port with four hundred men, two thirds of them dead drunk, below her decks.

The next day was calm, so calm that few got seasick, and with the whiskey gone, the gambling began. Sitting beside Jem, who seemed to have adopted him now that Con had apparently deserted him, Charley looked on as dicing and chuck-luck games played on a cloth took over the huge deck. Living in the Bowery, Charley had seen gambling before—but never anything like this. Soldiers gambled like madmen, losing their bounty pay to professional gamblers who had come aboard in New York, disguised as soldiers.

During the two days it took the steamer to travel down the Atlantic coast and into Chesapeake Bay, the men were kept below decks. Along with them, Charley Quinn saw nothing but dirty, disheveled Union soldiers and heard men cursing their luck in gambling or snoring in heavy sleep in the poisonous air. When not sleeping himself, Charley sat beside Jem, sharing his biscuits, cooked beef, and cheese rations but eating little so as not to anger the man.

He'd talked more to the printer, asking him questions. He'd learned that many of the men were what Jem called "bounty jumpers," men who had gone to enlistment offices in any number of towns and received cash bounties, then run off with the money to enlist somewhere else for more money. Weary of such practices, the Army now sent new troops to their destinations under guard so the men could not run off. If they tried to, they were shot at once.

Charley mourned Con. In all that time, Sullivan had not come near him. Johnny's "friend" had slept for twenty-four hours, then gambled constantly the rest of the time. He never came back to Charley to get his jacket, either, which Charley now wore for warmth in the sea dampness. It was as if Con had forgotten him and the jacket as well.

By now, the word was about below decks that their destination was a town called Alexandria, a seaport in a part of the state of Virginia that the Union Army had gained some time past. Charley had come to the South, all right, but what lay ahead for him here? The boy wondered anxiously what was to become of him now that every hour of sailing took him ever farther from the Bowery. What would happen when he had to leave the steamer? He'd surely be spotted for what he was.

Needing some kind of answer, Charley asked Jem what he thought the Army might do with him.

Jem's thoughtful reply chilled him to the heart. "Maybe some officer'll take you on as his servant, his striker—to help him pull his boots on and off. They won't take you as a soldier unless you be sixteen."

A *servant*? Charley cursed Con Sullivan under his breath. Mother Mary, no—never a servant! How could he avenge Johnny as a servant?

3 THE MAJOR AT THE WHARF

Although he could see nothing, Charley knew when the steamer had reached her destination by her slowing and the greeting whistles blasting from other ships in the port.

As the vessel prepared to dock on the fourth day of the voyage, Con Sullivan came shambling through the gloom toward him. Standing over Charley and Jem, he said, "I gotta have my jacket back now."

Without getting up, Charley slid out of the too large jacket and handed it to the man who had been so friendly to him in New York.

Jem Miller asked accusingly, "What do you plan to do with this boy now that we're here, Con? You told him to come along in New York."

Con shook his head. "I dunno. I was drunk that night." He grinned. "Anyhow, I got ye outa New York, Charley."

Charley was too disgusted to speak, but Jem went on talking. "We saw you playing chuck-luck. Got any money left to send Charley here back home on the railroad or a steamer? Or did you lose it all?"

Con sat down with a sigh. "The truth is, I lost it—lost every red cent of the bounty money. There were real gamblers aboard, and they cleaned me and some of the others out. Have ye got enough, Jem, to send him home? If ye do, I guess I'll have to owe ye."

Miller said flatly, "I never got any bounty money, and I left what money I had with my wife. What do you think'll happen to Charley?"

Sullivan shrugged. "He could join up here as easy as anywhere else."

Jem scoffed, "He's only twelve years old, Con. The way I see it, all he can be is an officer's servant."

Con shrugged again. "Well, anyway, that gets him away from the trouble he had in New York." Now Con fumbled about and took an apple from his haversack with the words, "Here's an apple for ye, Charley. Mebbe ye shouldn' have asked to come along with us."

When Charley didn't reach out for the apple, Con took a knife from his pocket, opened it, and sliced it in two. At the sight of the blade, Charley tensed. Sure as could be, it was his brother Johnny's fine staghorn one, a Christmas gift from him and Noreen. It had gone to Gettysburg with him.

Charley asked softly, "Where'd you get that knife, Con?"

The man stared at it for a moment, folded it, and put it back into his trousers pocket. Then he said, "I won it shootin' dice up in Pennsylvania."

"It was my brother's!" accused Charley. "He wouldn't gamble with it, not a Christmas gift."

"Well, I won it fair and square from him." Con scowled.

"But you brought back his silver watch."

Con nodded. "Why shouldn't I? He said he had a pretty sister, and I wanted to get a look at her. Besides, I got a gold watch of my own." He sighed. "Until yesterday I had it."

He took the knife off Johnny when he died, thought Charley, who now touched his brother's precious silver pocket watch in his left side pocket. If Johnny's watch had been a better one than Con's, it probably would not have come back to him and Noreen, either. And to think they had made so much of Sullivan, entertaining him at supper in an oyster house and holding him in high esteem. How wrong they had been about this man!

Charley mumbled, "I don't want your apple. I don't want to have anything to do with you anymore."

Sullivan got up and began to eat the apple. As he walked away, he said over his shoulder, "Suit yerself, kid. It ain't any skin off my nose if ye don't. Jest don't expect me to do ye no favors from now on. I don't need no Bowery brats hangin' around me."

"And I sure don't need you," muttered Charley under his breath. He scrambled to his feet and ran after Sullivan to say, "I'm gonna write my sister and tell her all about you so she'll know you ain't no hero."

"Go on, do it. Squawk to anybody ye want to. Tell the guards how I got ye aboard here. Now that we're here, they won't care. Nobody cares about the likes of ye. We're here to fight a war, not wipe noses."

Stung by this, Charley went back to Jem, who was now

standing and getting his equipment together to leave the ship.

"Can I come with you, Jem?" the boy asked.

Jem's smile was melancholy. "I'm afraid you can't, Charley. We'll be marched under guard so these bounty hunters won't get the chance to run. It's daylight now, so you'd be seen if I tried to hide you. You ought to go off last. Then you find yourself an officer and tell him how you got here and what you were up to."

"Ought I tell him Con Sullivan did it?"

"Why bother? All he has to do is say he didn't, and he'd say that, too."

"He said nobody cared about me here."

"That's about the truth of it, son."

Charley held out his hand. "Thank you for sharing your food with me and for talking to me. Maybe we'll meet up again wherever the 140th New York goes."

"Maybe so, Charley. Here's my hand on it and good luck to you."

Some minutes later, Charley heard the thud as the steamer's side met the wharf and the shouts of the deckhands as she was made fast. Almost immediately afterward, one of the guards at the bottom of the steps shouted out, "Find your regiment. Stay together and form in single file."

In the confusion of the moving soldiers seeking their regimental units, Charley lost sight of Jem Miller. He stood where he was while a strong-lunged guard called off the regiments by number and they marched up the companionway.

Within ten minutes' time, Charley Quinn was the

only one left in the large, murky, vile-smelling between-decks hold that had previously contained several hundred men. He felt lost, deserted.

A voice hailed him. "Who's that down there? Come here, soldier."

"I ain't no soldier," cried Charley. Then he came slowly forward to face a stern-faced, gray-bearded sergeant standing at the foot of the stairs.

"Who would you be?" demanded the soldier.

"Charles Quinn from New York City. I want to enlist, sir."

"*Enlist?*" The sergeant laughed. "You came all the way to Virginia to enlist? You could've done it on Chambers Street in New York and gotten bounty money for it." He peered down through the tobacco-heavy fog. "You're mighty small, ain'tcha? Are you old enough?"

"I think so," lied Charley. "I can already shoot."

"Well, whatever and whoever you are, you'll be goin' topside with me right now. You can't stay down here." And the man grabbed Charley by the shoulder.

Propelled onto the deck by the sergeant, Charley found his eyes dazzled by the clear, cool morning sunshine. The freshness of the salt air made him sneeze. He looked around at the blue harbor, busy with ships of every description: sailing ships at wharf with naked masts bare of sails, and ships entering under full sail; paddle-wheel, side-wheel, and propeller steamers; rowboats; and barges. The wharves were a hive of activity. Carts and wagons took on crates stacked up on the pier and unloaded others while carriages moved among them. Men, most of them in blue Yankee uniforms, pushed about, shouting and gesturing. Not far from the wharf stood a train made up of boxcars, its engine spouting steam as if it were impatient to leave. Long lines of blue-clad soldiers were heading toward the train two by two, the men who had just disembarked from the steamer.

The sergeant led Charley over to a tall, black-bearded man with the straps of an officer on his shoulders. Charley did not know his rank but did know enough to call him "sir." In his hands this officer held a board with papers on it.

"Major Caswell," said the sergeant, "this is what I found below when all the troops marched off."

"What is it? A stowaway?" asked the major.

"I think so."

"What sort of costume is he wearing?" asked the officer, looking at Charley's Bowery Boy uniform. "Who are you? Why were you with those soldiers?"

Charley took off his plug hat. The major had a heavy face and a frown to match it. "I'm Charles Quinn, sir, from New York City. This is what boys who live in the Bowery wear. I came to join the Army. I want to join the 140th New York Veterans Volunteers, my brother's regiment."

"Did your brother smuggle you aboard?"

"No, sir. He got killed at Gettysburg at Round Top."

The major's face softened now. He asked in a gentler tone, "How old are you?"

Relieved that he hadn't had to explain how he really got aboard, Charley tried a bold lie. "Sixteen."

"No! You're not even fourteen if you're a day. You have to be a full sixteen to enlist. Go back to New York."

"I can't. I haven't got any money but sixty cents, sir."

Over Charley's head, Major Caswell asked the sergeant, "Maybe the captain of some vessel will let him work his passage back as a cabin boy. There's nothing like an army to attract boys and dogs. On the other hand—" Suddenly the man looked down at Charley and asked, "Would you be Irish?"

"Oh, yes, sir, I am."

"Most Irish can sing. Can you?"

Astonished, Charley only gaped at the major. What a strange question!

The man went on, "Well, can you carry a tune?"

Charley nodded. "The sisters wanted to make a choirboy out of me, but I wouldn't be one. They said I had a good enough soprano, but I thought I sounded like a girl." Charley thought wistfully now of his school and how he'd refused to sing in the church choir because the Bowery Boys had laughed when he told them about it. Refusing the offer had made Noreen cry. He said, "I can carry a tune, sir."

"If you are musically inclined, I may know what to do with you." The officer turned the pages on his board to the last sheet, nodded, and said, "The Army is often in need of musicians. There may be a place for you, after all, in the First Division. That's where your 140th New York is."

Charley asked anxiously, "Do servants in the Army have to sing, sir?"

This made the major laugh again. "Not necessarily, though it helps to entertain when camp life gets too dull."

31

Why would the Army want a singer? Charley asked himself. Aloud he asked, "Will I have to take men's boots off, sir?"

"Not unless it suits you to do so for some officer at the headquarters company. I see by this that several regiments including the 140th New York are in need of a drummer. There didn't seem to be any aboard this ship—or buglers, either. I had hoped there might be some musicians in this latest batch of bounty jumpers. Now, truthfully, how old are you?"

"Twelve going on thirteen," Charley replied, and asked hopefully, "I'm not too young to be a drummer, am I?"

"No, you are the right age."

Charley's heart leapt, then he said truthfully once again, "But, sir, I don't know how to play a drum."

"You will be taught—if they decide to take you on. That is not up to me to decide."

"Where will I be going?"

Major Caswell pointed to the train. "With them. Now get over there and get aboard." The officer motioned to a private nearby. "Private Bradley, tell the officer in charge that this boy is a new recruit of sorts."

"Am I in the Army now?" Charley dared to ask.

"More or less, so far as I am concerned," replied the major, smiling down at Charley's joyful face.

Consumed with a desire to hug the officer and jump up and down for happiness, Charley fought back the urge. He asked, "Do drummers and buglers get to fight?"

Not one of the three soldiers present replied, although all three smiled as they looked at one another over his head. "Come along with me, boy," ordered the young private, who started off swiftly toward the waiting train with Charley half running at his side.

As they approached the train, Charley noted that each car had armed soldiers seated atop it. The door of the very last car stood open with guards in front of it. The private lifted Charley and pitched him inside. Then the door slid shut.

The car was crowded with sitting and leaning soldiers who made room for him with ill-grace. "My Gawd, it's a Bowery Boy!" exclaimed one, a little soldier with a pinched face. "What's he doin' here so far from home?"

Charley was proud to be recognized as being from the Bowery. As he lowered himself to the floor of the swaying, jolting car, he said, "I'm going to be a bugler or drummer boy."

"I hate buglers," came from another soldier. "They get us up in the mornings and put us to bed at night like we was mollycoddled babies."

Charley looked around the thronged car for Jem Miller but didn't see him. He would have preferred to be in Jem's car. He said, "When we stop, I'm going to get down and look for my friend's car so I can get in it with him."

"No, you won't," said the pinch-faced soldier. "We've all been warned. If we try to get out, we're gonna get shot down. Them guards are bound and determined that no bounty jumpin' goes on here."

Charley asked, "Are you part of the 140th New York?"

"Not us," said the soldier who hated buglers. "All of us in here are the 11th New York Battery. We're light artillery. The 140th is infantry, foot soldiers."

"I'm with the 140th. I volunteered," Charley said proudly.

The little pinch-faced man guffawed. "You'd have to do that. You're too much of a sprat to be drafted. How old are you, Bowery Boy, nine or ten?"

"Near to thirteen," replied Charley angrily.

"Well, if I was from the 140th, I'd send you back home to sprout up some. A bugle'll be almost as long as you are, and you can hardly be spotted over a drum, little feller."

Charley, not liking this kind of teasing, cried hotly, "Major Caswell said I was big enough."

"Who's Major Caswell, kid? He don't cut no ice with me."

Another Yankee put in, "Oh, leave him alone, Joshua. If he wants to join the Army, that's his bus'ness. He'll be sorry soon enough, once he gets a taste of what it's like bein' ordered around all day. Let's have us some music, Clem."

As a soldier began to play a harmonica, the men fell silent to listen.

Charley Quinn pondered the words he had heard from the major and these soldiers. Of course, he would get a uniform. He'd seen buglers and drummers at the head of military parades in New York City. They had looked splendid. Of course, he'd like the Army camp. Hadn't the major said that boys and dogs liked the Army? Maybe he could get a dog of his own when they got to the camp. He'd never owned one. It would be fine to see Jem Miller again and strut past Con Sullivan with a big dog at his heels as the drummer boy of the 140th New York. Come to think of it, there hadn't been a drummer boy in the parade Con and Jem had marched in—just a brass band that stayed behind on the wharf when the troops boarded the steamer.

Johnny's regiment would find out what a dandy soldier boy they had gotten in his younger brother—already a good shot and a fine fighter.

As he daydreamed about his glorious future in the Army, Charley listened to the quiet talk of the artillery-men standing near him. A big soldier who was pulling on his briar pipe so deeply that he was wreathed in blue smoke said, "I got good ears, better than most, and I overheard somethin' very interesting before we boarded. Guess who's at the town of Culpeper Courthouse, which ain't far from where we're headed at Brandy Station?"

"Abe Lincoln?" asked another man with a sharp laugh.

"No, not Abe. Gen'ral Meade, who whipped the Rebels at Gettysburg. And that sure as the devil ain't all who's there right now."

"Who else?" asked another soldier. "P. T. Barnum and all his elephants?"

"No, not him. Gen'ral Grant, Ulysses S. Grant, who's been fightin' and winnin' in the west. He's at Culpeper, too. Now what do you suppose it means when two big gen'rals get their heads together in the same place?"

The little pinch-faced soldier who had teased Charley put in softly, "I always say you can never tell which way a pickle's gonna squirt, but I'd say we're headed for a scrap. Do you suppose the Confederates know about this?"

"Sure they know. Rebels are supposed to be right here in Virginia, too, at a place called Orange. That ain't too far from where we're bound. This is their part of the country. There's plenty of Virginia folks around here that are civil to us and then run with messages to that old Confederate gen'ral Robert E. Lee, to tell him what we're up to. I bet when the scrap comes, he'll be ready and waitin'."

Charley Quinn drank up the words. A *scrap*? A *battle*! Sure there'd be one if two famous generals were both at the same place.

The pipe-smoking artilleryman went on in a deep rumble, "Think about somethin' else, too. It ain't only that them two are here together. It's comin' onto spring-time now. That's when the fightin' always starts up all over again, ain't it?"

4 CULPEPER

A couple hours' rattling over the rails brought the troop train to Brandy Station, Virginia, a camp of hundreds of white tents, where the Army of the Potomac had spent the winter. The artillerymen, with Charley Quinn last in line, jumped down from the car as soon as the door was unlocked. They marched off to their units at the Brandy Station camp under guard, but Charley, not knowing what to do except marvel at the sight of rows and rows of tents, waited beside the train.

Beckoned over by an officer, he had to explain who he was, why he was there, and what the major in Alexandria had told him.

This officer, another major, nodded, stared silently up and down at Charley's black-and-red Bowery Boy clothing, and pointed toward a group of guards just ahead near the locomotive. He said, "The men in boxcar number three are the regiment you want. Go up there and tell the guards they're to open that car and put you inside. You'll be bound for their headquarters company."

"What's that? Headquarters?" asked Charley.

"That's where the colonel of the New York 140th will be. He's not here in Culpeper."

Charley's eyes widened at the thought of seeing a real live colonel.

The officer laughed at his odd expression. "Colonels bark but don't generally bite if you hop to when they bark."

Charley asked, "Will I see General Meade?"

"Perhaps, if you keep your eyes open. I'm busy now, lad. I can't stay here with you. Do as I say." And with that the major walked away hastily toward the waiting train.

Charley ran to the designated boxcar and told the guards what the major had said. He waited till the door was unlocked and pulled open just wide enough for him to squeeze inside. Then he was boosted up by a big guard into the crowded car.

A shout went up from one of the men in the car. "Hey, it's that Bowery Boy we took on in New York. Hey, Con, it's your chum!"

"No chum a mine," rumbled Sullivan, who stood not far from Charley. "Shove him over to Jem Miller. He's got himself a corner."

Pushed by many hands, Charley was propelled roughly along, even lifted into the air at times, through the car to various corners. Finally, in the fourth corner, he came to the spot where Miller sat. Jem grinned at him and said, "So you got here, after all?"

"You bet. I'm to be a bugler or a drummer boy if the 140th'll have me."

Jem patted him on the back as the boy knelt. "Well, you wanted to come. I hope you get to be what you want."

"Did you ever play an instrument, Jem?"

"Not one time, Charley. I can't carry a tune in a potato sack."

Charley told the man excitedly, "General Meade and General Grant are both in Culpeper. Somebody out of the 11th New York Battery told me. I was in their boxcar first."

"Were you now? That's news about the generals."

"He said their being together down here meant a battle."

"Charley, I do believe it does." Jem's voice was deeper and his face hard-set. "If that old buzzard Meade had followed up the Rebels after the Battle of Gettysburg, he could have ended this confounded war last year. We wouldn't be down here to fight again, and I could be back in my print shop in Elmira right now."

"Maybe we'll end it here," came from Charley.

"I dunno, boy. This is Confederate home ground. They know every road and cow path, and we don't. They'll fight like devils for their own land. And if you want to take a gander at what they're fighting to hold on to, look out this knothole here and get a view of some country. I been looking myself. You'll find it different from what you're used to."

Squirming about to make himself comfortable, Charley sat down and put one eye to the hole. Never in his life had he seen such greenness, as trees, meadows, and hillsides flickered past outside the train. It was as if the

Central Park he knew had been expanded hundreds of times. Now and then he caught sight of a windowless redbrick structure, burned-out skeletons of houses, or half-burned cabins. Once he saw a ragged-looking black man on the seat of a mule-drawn wagon waiting at a crossing as the troop train clicked past. He figured this man must have been a slave until the previous year, when Abe Lincoln had set him and all the other slaves in the South free.

Slavery! Anger rose up in Charley at the very thought of the word. Johnny and Noreen had hated the idea, and the sisters had spoken against it in school. No person should ever be owned by any other person!

After a half hour's ride, the train stopped, and the 140th New York got down in Culpeper, some sixty miles from Alexandria. It had to be the smallest place Charley Quinn had ever set eyes on—just a few brick buildings and brick and frame houses set in rows with gardens out front. Beyond, to the west, were mountain peaks visible as a blue mass and, below them, farms and forests.

Charley had to admit that the camp around the town was big, though. It was a whole city itself, an Army town with long streets of tents and log cabins covered with canvas cloth. The muddy avenues were clogged with riders, wagons, horses, and mules—as busy as Broadway had always been at home. On the plain before the camp, he saw columns of soldiers marching back and forth, their feet churning mire under a cloudy sky filled with hundreds of black crows. Never before had he seen so many birds at one time, nor so many dogs running about!

The major at the wharf had been right about the dogs. The camp was one great clamor of birds cawing, dogs barking, officers shouting loud-voiced commands, horses nickering and clopping their hooves, wagon wheels constantly screeching.

As he stood looking about, Charley heard a guard bellow, "You recruits of the 140th New York, fall in by fours."

"Fall in behind us," Jem told Charley.

"What does that mean?"

"Get in a line. March behind us until you see our headquarters. Then stop there."

"Will I see you again, Jem?"

"Sure, you will."

Charley waited till the soldiers formed in columns and set off. Then he came in behind them, running to keep up. Officers riding past smiled at him, but he didn't see them. He was where he wanted to be. With Johnny's regiment!

When the 140th was marched down a street of tents and told to halt, Charley halted, too. He waited until the men were checked off by name and assigned to a company and a tent. Then his turn came.

A big, red-faced sergeant with an Irish accent asked him, "Who the devil would ye be, Bowery Boy? Take off yer hat and tell me."

As Charley removed his hat, he said, "Charles Stephen Quinn, sir. I'm to be a bugler or drummer boy. I hear you need one. My brother was Johnny Quinn. Did you know him?"

"Indeed. What a hell-raiser he was, too! Come along

with me to headquarters and we'll see what's to be done with ye."

As Charley started away beside the long-shanked man, he asked, "Do you truly need a bugler or drummer here?"

The sergeant nodded. "We do. Our drummers and buglers take turns of duty. Watch where ye go. Don't fall over that tent line with yer big feet. The officers will deal with ye, not me."

More officers? He was afraid of them, but all the same, he followed the sergeant hopefully.

Ten minutes' walk over red earth took them past a brick courthouse and a steepled church to the veranda-shaded Virginia Hotel. The hitching rack in front of the hotel was filled with horses and young officers waiting beside their mounts. Guards with muskets paced back and forth on the veranda.

Walking past the soldiers, Charley and the sergeant entered a hall outside a small room, which at one time must have been the hotel office. Two boys in blue uniforms sat there side by side on a bench. One was plump and dark and had a gleaming bugle in his lap. The other, a tall, thin, freckly boy, had a small drum beside him, and drumsticks stuck in his belt. A drummer boy! So there was no need for him, after all. Charley's heart sank as he waited with them.

The sergeant who had brought him here had gone into the small room and now returned and beckoned him with a crooked finger.

There at a desk in the bare room sat a lanky, yellow-haired officer. Hunched over the desk, he was busy with papers spread out before him. Finally, he looked up as the sergeant said, "Captain Mahoney, I fetched ye a replacement for young Gorman, sir. This boy wants to join the 140th for special reasons."

"Does he? Well, call Gorman inside, then." The captain's voice was low and sounded as if he had a head cold.

Sticking his head outside the door, the sergeant yelled, "Gorman, you, the drummer of the day, git in here!"

A moment later the tall, freckled boy was standing in the doorway saluting the captain.

"Gorman," asked the officer, "are you truly sixteen years of age now?"

"Yes, sir, last week. I'm old enough to be a real soldier now. It's time for me to stop drumming," said Gorman, whose voice had a man's depth.

The officer frowned and said, "Soldiering has to come a bit later for you, I'm afraid. By rights the band drum major should teach this boy, but he's got camp fever. Can you show him how to use your drum in a month's time? You'll have the mornings free for teaching."

"I think I can, sir, in the mornings, if he's foxy and applies himself."

"Are you smart and will you work hard?" the captain asked Charley.

"Yes, sir, I'll sure try."

"All right, then. Gorman, you'll sign your enlistment papers as soon as I have them ready for you. Tomorrow morning you'll begin to teach this boy to beat a drum, and you'll drill with the men in the afternoons yourself. Teach this lad everything he needs to know about his duties as a drummer boy."

"I will, sir."

43

Now the captain turned to Charley. "What is your name?"

"Charley Quinn, sir."

"A good Irish name. We are mostly Irish here." The officer smiled up at Charley. "Work hard and we'll see to it that you get a drummer boy's uniform. Would you like that?"

"Oh, yes, I would!"

"Well, then, welcome to the 140th New York. You'll be paid thirteen dollars a month, not by Abe Lincoln as soldiers are but by the officers here."

Charley nodded happily. He said, "My brother, John Francis Quinn, served with you until Gettysburg. He got killed there at Round Top."

The captain's face changed. "Yes, I knew him. He got into lots of trouble, but he was a brave man."

"He was a Bowery Boy like me," Charley said proudly.

Now the lanky officer grew stern. "You're not a Bowery Boy now! Get rid of that red shirt and that plug hat. They won't do here at all. Gorman, find him another shirt and a soldier's cap at once. We'll take the Bowery Boy out of you soon enough."

Charley caught his breath. Clearly, the captain didn't favor his gang. Did the Dead Rabbits predominate here among the New York soldiers? He asked, "Are there lots of Dead Rabbits here, sir?"

Captain Mahoney replied, "I know all about your gangs, because I'm a New Yorker, too. We have no Bowery Boys here that I know of right now. There are some Dead Rabbits, but they behave themselves now. I warn you. Put your New York City rioting behind you or you'll fare the worse for it. Our punishments are not light. We are here to fight the Rebels, not each other. Now, Gorman, take him and outfit him."

"Thank you, sir," said Charley, not too happy with the scolding and realizing it would be hard to give up his Bowery Boy clothing. He waited to see if he was to sign some papers, too, but he saw the officer turn his attention to a long list of names in front of him. It was time to leave with the boy named Gorman.

Outside, Gorman introduced himself as Silas and the bugler of the day as Tom Fallon. Then, beckoning with his finger, Gorman invited Charley to follow him down a long, cool, dimly lit corridor with doors on either side. One near Captain Mahoney's office opened into a large, lavishly furnished room. It was the lobby of the hotel. Sentries with bayonet-tipped muskets stood on each side of the door, and inside a number of Union officers were gathered in a circle in chairs. The air was gray-blue with the smoke of their cigars and pipes.

Gorman spoke to one of the sentries, who nodded agreement to what he had said. Then the boy took Charley by the coat sleeve and whispered into his ear. "There they are. Go closer and take a look at General Grant and General Meade."

Generals? Real generals? Fascinated at the idea of seeing great men he'd only read about in New York City newspapers, Charley came nearer and stared into the big room. He asked softly, so as not to be heard, "Which one of them is General Grant?"

"Grant's a lieutenant general. He's the sort of heavyset one with the dark beard at the very end. He's wearin' a real plain uniform, a private's coat it is, but the three stars on his shoulder boards show that he's a general. All generals wear stars, but other than that, they can wear whatever they want to wear."

Surprised that anyone would want to dress like a private, the lowest Army rank—like Johnny had been—Charley was now curious to see what General Meade looked like. "Which one's Meade?" he asked.

Gorman pointed. "The one in the red chair next to Grant. He's the one with the big nose and straggly hair. He has on spectacles."

"What's he like?"

"He's a powerful cusser, but he's a fair man, all the same. He's been wounded lots a times, but he always comes back for more fightin'!"

A sharp whisper from the sentry sent Gorman farther down the corridor. At the end, he opened a door and went outside. Before them was a low brick house with chimneys sending up smoke. Gorman said now, "We're goin' to see Marcus. Are you hungry?"

"You bet. Who's Marcus?"

"He's the officers' cook. He used to be a slave who lived not far from here. He got 'emancipated' and left the master he had cooked for to cook for us. He's a friend of mine. He's the best cook in Virginia. The officers pay him real good. Come on. You let me do the talking to Marcus." Gorman chuckled. "Most soldiers eat beans and bacon, but when we get duty up here at the hotel, we eat just fine."

Following the other boy, Charley walked into the big cook house where a large black man and three black boys about Gorman's age worked busily, chopping, stirring, and kneading food at large tables and shining stoves.

The big man looked up from chopping meat, raised his knife, and pointed it at Gorman and Charley. He thundered in a bass voice, "How many times have I told ya there's to be no Lincoln soldiers in my kitchen!"

"But I only came for a soda-powder biscuit and butter." Gorman spoke in a high, wheedling tone.

"All winter long you allus knew where to find 'em, boy."

"And some honey?"

"You know where that's kept, too." As Gorman got two biscuits out of a large basket and spread them with butter and some honey, Marcus asked Charley with mock ferocity, "Who'd you be, redheaded devil boy?"

"The new drummer for the 140th New York."

"Mighty puny, ain'tcha?"

"Gorman don't think I am, and neither does Captain Mahoney."

"Who said they has good sense? I got better things to do than fool with boys. Git out of my way, both of ya."

"Thanks, Marcus. We'll be back." With a laugh, Gorman gave Charley a biscuit. Then he broke into a run with Charley following behind, eating the light-as-air biscuit.

Gorman didn't return to the hotel. Instead, he slowed to a walk and turned down a street of cabins topped with canvas. As they walked, Gorman said, "I been with the 140th as a drummer ever since it was first started up in 1862, when I was fourteen. I lived on a farm in Brooklyn till then. My uncle brought me into this outfit with him.

He got bunged up so bad at Gettysburg, he couldn't come back to the regiment. He lost a leg, you see."

Charley frowned, thinking of what he had lost there. He asked, "Did you know my brother, Johnny? He got killed there along with Colonel O'Rourke."

"Not too good. He never paid me any heed."

Charley nodded and next asked, "Did you know Con Sullivan?"

"You bet." Gorman paused to fix Charley with bright hazel eyes. "Your brother was a friend of his. Sullivan ain't worth much as a soldier. Good riddance to him is what I said after Gettysburg."

Charley said with a laugh, "Well, you got him back now. He even got paid bounty money to come back to the 140th."

Gorman groaned as he ducked into the open doorway of a cabin with a split-log floor. He said, "Somebody would have had to pay Sullivan to get him here."

Charley confided, "My sister and I thought he was a real hero when he fetched Johnny's watch back to us after he got killed."

"I'm surprised he fetched it back at all. Sullivan's got a line of blarney. Now, what do you think of where we bunk?"

Charley looked around him at a fireplace, table, some old wooden chairs, and some bunks set into the walls.

Gorman pointed. "That bunk is where you'll sleep. I sleep over there, this is Fallon's bunk, and that's the captain's."

Surprised, Charley asked, "Does *he* sleep in here with us?"

"Uh-huh. The other officers are billeted at the hotel, but there ain't room for all of 'em. Captain Mahoney ain't too bad for a shoulder straps."

"Could I have a dog?" asked Charley.

"No, the captain already told Fallon no. Tom had one that was full of fleas."

To hide his disappointment Charley changed the subject. "What else do I do besides beat on a drum?"

"Lots of things. Carry water, draw maps, help the surgeons sharpen their instruments, tend to the wounded in battle—and other things. Say, can you cut hair?"

When Charley shook his head no, Gorman smiled. "Drummer boys cut hair usually. I'm good at it by now. I'll teach you how, maybe. And once you know how to beat out the everyday camp calls, you might play in the fife and bugle corps or the band we got here. Fallon's a jim-dandy bugler by now. He had plenty of time to learn, though." Gorman's face grew serious. "I ain't got a lot of time to teach you in if it's only a month we've got. I ought to have six months."

"Why only a month, then?"

Gorman was rubbing the fuzz on his chin. "That's what I want to know. I've got a good idea, though. With Grant's coming here, I think we'll be having ourselves a fight pretty soon. The Army of Northern Virginia ain't too far from Culpeper right at this very minute."

"What's that?" asked Charley.

"We're the Army of the Potomac. The Johnny Rebs call themselves the Army of Northern Virginia. They got old Robert E. Lee with 'em, just like they had at Gettysburg. The way I see it, I got to learn to shoot a sight better'n I do now, and you got to learn how to beat a drum right, and neither of us got long to do it."

"Do I get to fight, too?" Charley asked hopefully.

"Not unless you quit drummin', pick up a musket from somebody else, and start shootin'. Drummer boys ain't supposed to fight."

"Did you fight at Gettysburg?"

Gorman shook his head. "No, I had chicken pox. I was sick in bed then."

Gorman now got down on his knees to rummage in a tin trunk. He came up with a gray shirt, which he handed to Charley with the words, "Wear this. It belongs to Fallon, but he won't care. It ought to fit you."

As Charley took the shirt and, with a pang of homesickness, began to put his own Bowery Boy clothing into the open trunk, he made a vow. He would quit drumming and pick up a musket for Johnny's sake as soon as he could.

5 LESSONS

After more rummaging in the trunk, Silas Gorman found a Union Army blue forage cap, an overlarge dark blue coat, and an even larger greatcoat for Charley. Charley could not see how he looked, but he hoped it was military.

Guessing what he was thinking, Gorman told him, "You look more like the Army now. Later on we'll get you some real shoes that don't have high heels."

"What do I do now, Silas?"

"Follow me around the rest of the day and see what I do. Tomorrow morning we'll start on the drum. The way we drum is danged important, Charley. Bugle calls and drumbeats are signals. No one person can run up to every man in a company or regiment and tell him what the captain wants him to do next. The calls tell them that. So they have to get heard by everybody. You got to work hard and learn fast and always be where the captain can find you when you're on duty. The army's no place for a deaf man, a lazy one, or a bad drummer."

"I'll try hard as I can."

"All right, let's go back to the hotel now. I can't be away from there too long, or the captain'll be sore at me. Besides, I want to make another raid on Marcus for more biscuits. Could you eat another one?"

"Oh, sure."

Tall Silas grinned. "Good. I like it when I get duty up at the hotel. Not only can I go see Marcus, I get to hear what comes over the telegraph from Abe Lincoln. We get messages from him all the time."

By following Gorman and listening to his drumbeats and doing the few camp errands he was given by his officer, Charley started his education at Culpeper. Before that first day was out, he also learned that there were indeed Dead Rabbits around, too. When soldiers fell out from their afternoon drilling at a bugle call, he stood with Gorman watching them come back wearily to their tents. Suddenly he spotted two young men walking together whom he knew to be members of the rival gang. One of them apparently recognized him, because he glared as Charley passed within an arm's length of him.

Silas saw the wicked look, too, and asked, "Do you know him, Charley?"

"He knows me, Silas. He used to be a Dead Rabbit. He and my brother used to fight each other in New York."

Gorman nodded. "That's Dan Whaley. Just before we were at Gettysburg, he fought your brother behind the privies."

"Did Johnny whip him?"

"Your brother was winnin'. But the officers got wind of

the fight and put a stop to it." Gorman's long face grew solemn. "They made 'em both stand on the chines for a long time."

"What's the chines?"

"Chines? The chines are sort of on a barrel. An empty barrel. A man being punished has to stand with one foot on one side of the barrel and the other on the other side. He stands there for hours over the empty space. Sounds easy to do, but after a while, it gets to hurtin' real bad, I hear. That's one comp'ny punishment. There are others. For somethin' real bad like desertin', the punishment is to get shot."

"Oh."

Gorman punched Charley gently. "Don't you worry. Dan Whaley won't pester you here, knowin' what'll happen to him if he does."

"I ain't afraid of him, Silas." All the same, Charley had to admit to himself that what the drummer boy had told him about his being safe was a comfort. After all, from what Captain Mahoney had said, he was the only Bowery Boy here.

Catching the look on Charley's face, Gorman told him, "If a drummer boy gets into trouble, his officer whales the tar out of him. Captain Mahoney's got a hard hand with a switch. I felt it one time."

"What'd you do that was bad?"

"I was late gettin' to where I was supposed to be with my drum, and I didn't have a good enough excuse. Let that be a warnin' to you. When you're supposed to be somewhere at a certain time in this Army, you better be there. It ain't like school here, where you can be tardy."

Charley smiled. For a fact, Gorman hadn't ever gone to school with the sisters he'd known in New York City. It was dangerous to be tardy with them. They boxed ears. He asked, "Will I get a real soldier's uniform as a drummer boy?"

"Not *just* like a soldier's but pretty close to it. You won't be a real soldier the way I'm goin' to be pretty soon."

Again Charley smiled. No, he'd be a real soldier, too! Everybody in the 140th New York was going to find out that Johnny Quinn's little brother was as full of vinegar and gunpowder as his brother had been. He pondered telling Silas how well he could shoot at a target but thought better of it. When the time came, his marksmanship would be a big surprise to everybody. He'd had a good look at the soldiers' muskets on the long trip down here. They were Springfields and Enfields, the kind he'd used at the shooting galleries back home. He knew how to use a ramrod and cartridges—how to load and fire—just about everything about muskets there was to know. All Bowery Boys knew those things.

That night, after a fine supper of Marcus's chicken in a back room of the hotel, Charley went out to find Jem Miller. He walked down the street of tents that housed the 140th New York, asking at tent after tent for the soldier by name. Finally, a grizzled corporal sitting on a keg smoking a pipe pointed to a tent near the end of the long line.

"There's somebody named Jem down there."

Jem was inside the tent folding some small pieces of clothing into his knapsack. Other men lounged around on their blankets, smoking and playing cards or reading Beadle's dime novels. As Charley walked over to him, he noticed that there were no bunks or beds or furniture around. Tents didn't look so good to him now as they had on the train. He was far better housed as a drummer boy than Jem was as a soldier.

Jem grinned a welcome. "Why, Charley, I hardly knew you out of your Bowery duds. What're you doing here? Did they take you on as a bugler?"

"No, they're taking me on as a drummer to this regiment, Jem." And Charley told the man of Gorman's turning sixteen and of his plans to start teaching him the drum the very next morning. He finished with, "He showed me General Meade and General Grant in a room up there in the hotel. I wasn't but twenty feet away from Grant."

Jem nodded. "That's probably the closest you'll ever get. Lots of times soldiers don't ever set eyes on a general unless he reviews a parade. You seem to be lucky, Charley. What're they paying you?"

"A whole thirteen dollars a month."

"Same as I get." Jem smiled. "What'll you do with all that money?"

"I think I'll send part of it home to my sister to keep for me. Can I do that?"

"Sure, you can send money home. That's smart thinking. Don't you think you ought to write to your sister? You left awful sudden. I've got some paper, an envelope, and a pencil here. I just wrote to my wife. The Army'll send your letter for free."

Charley bit his lower lip. Yes, he ought to write

Noreen so she'd stop worrying. She'd have the Metropolitans out looking for him by now. He said, "I guess I ought to write. Thank you, Jem."

"Well, sit down on my blanket roll and do it. It don't have to be long. One thing, though, Charley, you can't say where you are. That's the way the Army does it—to keep where we are secret."

"All right, Jem."

Sitting cross-legged on the blanket roll and using Jem's paper and pencil, Charley wrote:

Dear Noreen,

To make it easy on you to marry Mr. Demarest, I joined the Union Army and went off with them. I hope one of the Bowery Boys already told you this. They saw me go. You can stop hunting for me if you are maybe doing it. I met up with Con Sullivan again. He's no good. I doubt he ever was. He's got Johnny's knife. He says he won it off him gambling. I think he stole it. I can't tell you where I am, but they plan to make a drummer boy out of me here in Johnny's old regiment. I want to be a hero like him. Don't you worry about me. I can take care of myself. I got some friends and I eat good. Take care of yourself.

Love,
Charley

Folding the letter, the boy stuffed it into the envelope, addressed it, and gave it to Jem with the words, "I wish I could tell her we'll be having a scrap with the Rebs soon and that they're in a camp not too far away from where we are right now."

Jem shook his head. "I didn't tell my Lucy, either, and it wasn't because soldiers can't write secret things like that. It'd scare her and it'd scare your sister, too. The war's as hard on them as it is on us. It ain't fun to wait."

"I know what you mean about waiting, Jem. I can hardly wait to learn how to play a drum so that I can be a real soldier, too. Gorman is going to take a horse and wagon and two drums and me away from camp tomorrow to practice. Captain Mahoney told him he don't want me doing my first drumming where anybody'd hear me and get an earache."

This made Jem chuckle. "That's wise of the captain."

Charley asked, "Will we see any Confederates if we leave camp?"

"Not unless you travel almost due south of here to a place called Orange. But keep a keen eye out for any graybacks out scouting."

Charley vowed, "I'd surely like to see a Johnny Reb."

Jem said sadly, "I'm pretty sure we all will see some, and soon, too, Charley. Don't you be eager to. Did you know that the 146th New York is here in Culpeper, too?"

"Are they?" Charley's face lit up, hearing of the other regiment. "They were alongside us at Gettysburg, weren't they?"

"Yes, they were."

Charley thought for a moment, then asked, "Is Con Sullivan in this company, too?"

"No, this is Company A. He's in Company B."

Looking at the other men lounging about the tent, Charley asked in a whisper, "Are there any bounty jumpers in here?"

"Yes, a couple, but it doesn't matter now. There are

guards all over this camp day and night. There won't be much sneaking off right now. Maybe later on, though."

"When'll that be?" asked the boy.

"When they know for sure there's going to be a battle."

"Cowards!" spat Charley Quinn angrily. "Only cowards would desert."

"That's right, son."

Now Charley got to his feet and said, "I'd better get back before lights-out. Thanks for all your help, Jem." Jem nodded as Charley walked away.

After taps was blown by Tom Fallon, Charley lay down on a pine needle–filled mattress and fell asleep, contented with his new life.

The next day, following a five-in-the-morning roll call and a pancake breakfast, Charley and Silas headed out of camp with their drums.

On the way, Gorman told Charley the routine of the day. "There are a dozen calls you got to learn, Charley. First is reveille, which comes at dawn. At six-thirty, after breakfast, the soldiers clean up the camp and their quarters. The guard mounts at eight for their duty of the day guardin' the camp. At eight-thirty, the men drill on the parade ground till noon. After lunch, they have free time to write letters and things like that till two, and from two to three-thirty they drill some more. Then they're dismissed to get ready for retreat and dress parade. After that, at seven, they have supper, and at eight come tattoo and roll call again, and they go to their quarters. Nine o'clock comes taps and lights-out."

Charley volunteered, "At nine o'clock, the Bowery's

just getting warmed up for the night."

"That may be, but down here bedtime comes early."

Charley asked over the soft nicker of the horse Gorman was driving, "What do you have to learn to be a soldier?"

"Plenty. How to march forward and by the flank and obliquely and how to shift arms—the musket, I mean—how to fire standing, kneeling, and prone; and bayonet fighting. I'll drill and drill. Sundays I'll have to stand inspection with all my equipment cleaned up with spit and dust. Then that day I'll march out to the parade ground with my regiment, stack my musket with the other ones, and lay out my knapsack for the officers to poke around in and—"

Tired of this, Charley interrupted, "But you do get to fight?"

"Yes, I will, now that I'm not just a drummer boy."

Just a drummer boy! Charley fell silent while the wagon went slowly along the lines of tents and cabins and individual soldiers getting ready for the long morning drill that would turn them into an anonymous, many-legged, single unit.

Once they were into the woods, Gorman told Charley, "I'm takin' us to the place the captain took Fallon when he was learnin' the bugle calls. It's far enough away so nobody can hear you drummin'. We're goin' to the edge of the Wilderness."

Charley looked about him at the tall trees, soon to leaf out for spring, lining both sides of the wagon. There were more trees here in Virginia than he'd ever seen before in his whole life. Away from the camp, early-blooming wildflowers dotted the tall grass like tiny stars of many colors. Wasn't this a wilderness?

He asked, "What's *the* Wilderness?"

Gorman laughed sharply. "A special place. A god-awful place full of trees and brush and vines so thick, you can't see more'n a couple yards in front of you. They used to mine for iron in there a hundred years ago, and they cut down all the big trees to feed the fires they needed to smelt the iron. The trees that grew back once they stopped iron mining grew back real close together. You'll be seeing the edge of it today. Where we are right now ain't no wilderness at all, if that's what you're thinkin'." For a while Silas whistled, then he asked Charley, "Say, do you notice how different it is here in Virginia from New York City in the nighttime?"

Charley nodded his head. It seemed to him that he'd scarcely slept at all the night before for hearing birdcalls and strange, high-pitched piping noises. He tried to imitate the piping to Gorman.

He got a laugh in return. "I seen a lot of diff'rent birds down here I don't know the names of. Some of 'em even whistle back at you when you whistle to them. That high noise you heard comes from toads, little tiny ones. They're real early this year, says Captain Mahoney."

"Toads?" exclaimed Charley, who had never seen a toad.

"Hunderds and hunderds of 'em, Charley."

They rode the rest of the way in silence. Finally, Gorman pulled the horse to a halt, got out the drums and the sticks, and said, "Get down. I want to show you something before we start practicing."

Charley followed Gorman up a narrow dirt road,

bordered by many young trees growing close together with very heavy undergrowth beneath them, and stopped when he did.

Silas Gorman was staring at a wooden board on which letters had been scratched more than carved out: CORPORAL WILLIAM GARRETT, C.S.A.

Gorman said softly, "That's where a dead Rebel's buried, Charley. There are graves all over here, Yankee and Rebel. They're kind of shallow because they were dug in a hurry. People who come down here find bones and skulls and pieces of gray and blue uniforms."

"Was there a scrap here?"

"Yes, the battle of Chancellorsville was fought around here last year before Gettysburg. The Rebels won. Do you want to look around some? We got the time."

Even with his back warmed by the Virginia sunshine, Charley Quinn found himself shivering. "No thanks," he said. He didn't relish the thought of seeing skeletons and skulls. He wanted to ask Gorman to take him somewhere else, but if he did the other boy would think he was a coward. No, keeping quiet was best.

Gorman, who didn't seem to notice Charley's nervousness, attached one of the drums to the sash he wore and put the sticks into his belt. Then he put the other sash over Charley's head and attached an identical fourteen-inch-wide, twelve-inch-deep wooden-shell drum at his left hip. Handing Charley the sticks, he said, "First I'll go through the beats I use for the daily calls. Then I'll teach you the calls for 'forward,' 'rally,' and the commands you'll need to know when we go to fight. Do what I do after I do it. I ain't got much time to teach you, so pay attention. Some of the calls come easier than others."

Taking the sticks from Silas, Charley straightened up as tall as he could, steadying himself to learn to be the next drummer boy of the heroic and famous New York 140th.

But before he hit the drum for the very first time, he asked Silas, "Could a Confederate cavalry patrol hear us?" Silas had told him the Rebels were camped somewhere to the south, and he didn't want to see a Johnny Reb without a musket ready.

Gorman said matter-of-factly, "Maybe. They know the paths in and out of here. Nobody ever knows where cavalry is. They can come at you from anywhere. Our own cavalry, too. Just try not to think about 'em. Anyhow, Charley, the wind's blowin' toward the north, so that's where the sound'll carry. If it turns around and starts to blow south, we'll quit and get in the wagon and head for Culpeper.

"Now I'll show you how to do a ratamacus. Listen good and try it after me. Don't expect to sound just like I do right off."

Charley's hands were sweating, but he took a firm grip on the drumsticks and stood waiting for Silas Gorman, who gazed intently at him with lifted sticks before he brought them down on his own drum.

6 SANDERS FIELD

Each day for almost two months, Charley and his drum went out with a wagon to different spots in the Virginia countryside, but not always with Silas Gorman. Sometimes drummer boys from other divisions served as his teacher. In going to other parts of the war-torn state, Charley saw the damage from past fighting in the form of deserted, shell-marked houses; burned-out tobacco barns; and unplowed fields long gone to weeds. When he was with him, Silas told Charley what skirmishes had taken place there—if he knew.

Charley liked the other boys he met well enough and worked hard to learn what he could from them, but he made no real friends among them the way he had with Silas and Jem.

His newly made drummer's uniform was indeed splendid, and he always wore his drumsticks at his belt. He found he had natural rhythm, and his swift progress pleased Silas and Captain Mahoney. Keeping the sticks by him constantly, Charley beat on anything available in camp: walls, wooden floors, fences, wagon sides, and even once on a sergeant's broad back.

In all this time, he still scarcely knew Tom Fallon, the bugler. There was very little forthcoming from the boy. Charley wondered if Tom's silence was due to the fact that he stuttered. It was hard for him to get words out. Silas said that Tom "talked with his trumpet," not his mouth.

In the weeks Charley spent learning his job in the Army, he saw Jem Miller two more times, each time between tattoo and taps. Jem, a corporal now, was as pleasant as always, and ever glad to see him.

One time only, the boy saw Con Sullivan, and that time was ugly. Driving out in a wagon to practice with a Third Division drummer boy, Charley spotted Con standing under an oak with soldiers holding muskets with fixed bayonets surrounding him. Con himself was weaponless.

The drummer boy stopped the wagon and told Charley, "That soldier's gonna get punished."

"Is he?"

"You bet. I bet he cussed out an officer or stole somethin'. Let's watch it."

Seated next to the other lad, Charley looked on as Sullivan's arms were jerked up by two burly soldiers and ropes were fastened around his hands and fingers. The ropes were thrown over the low limb of the tree, and Con was pulled up until he stood on his tiptoes only, with his weight on his thumbs.

The other drummer said matter-of-factly, "Strung up by the thumbs. They'll leave him like that for a while till he learns his lesson."

"I know him," Charley told the boy. "He was with my brother when he got killed at Gettysburg."

"Well, don't try to cut him down or you'll get thrashed."

"I won't. I didn't say I liked him, did I?"

"No. Let's get going."

As the two drummer boys passed in their wagon, Sullivan spotted Charley. At the top of his lungs, he yelled, "I see ye, Charley Quinn. Look yer fill, ye dirty little guttersnipe."

After the other drummer boy had clucked to the startled horse to go on, he said, "It appears to me he don't like you, either."

Charley answered, "For a fact, he don't. He likes whiskey better'n anything else."

"He ain't alone here in favorin' whiskey," came from the other boy.

That was true. In the short time he'd been with the Army, Charley had noticed how much gambling went on and how much whiskey made its way into the camp.

On the morning of April seventeenth, Gorman went out again with Charley and, after putting him through his paces drumming, he said, "You're doin' fine. Keep at it. Practice all the time. Beat on anythin' that'll stand still for you. Sleep with your drum beside you at nights, and don't ever go anyplace without it. I'd say by the first of May you'll be ready to do my old job even if you ain't ready to play in the brass band at dress parade. Men'll understand what you're beatin' out. You're a real jim-dandy. You sure took to this natural-like. It took me six months to learn what you know now. And you already know everythin' you'll need. I'm proud of you, Charley Quinn."

And Charley blushed with pleasure and joy.

That same night, Silas came running to the cabin with important news he'd heard at the hotel. General Meade had sent special orders to Washington, D.C., asking for large supplies of wagons, medicines, and food. To boot, he'd requested fifty rounds of ammunition for every soldier. He wanted every man in his command to have six days' rations of food and another ten days' supply to be carried on wagons. There was also to be ten days' supply of grain for cavalry and wagon mules and horses. In three days' time, Meade wanted to have four thousand wagons ready to drive off at an hour's notice.

"Sure as can be," said Gorman, "we're gonna be movin' out of Culpeper."

"Where to?" asked Charley.

"To where we can find General Lee and his Rebs."

"Can I go tell a friend of mine?" Charley looked to Captain Mahoney now, who was in the room with them.

"Sure. I bet he knows already. Nothing on earth moves faster than news in an army camp."

As the captain had predicted, Jem Miller already had the news. He was darning one of his socks by lantern light and greeted Charley with, "I can tell from your face that you heard what happened."

"I sure have. When'll we be leaving?"

"Not right this minute. Sit down."

Charley sat on a home-fashioned stool facing Jem,

who sat on its exact counterpart. "Well, when will we go?" he repeated.

"When the generals decide. When we're told to cook enough meat for several days' eating, clean our muskets well, and be sure to have forty rounds of cartridges in our cartridge boxes and the other ten in our pockets or knapsacks. That's when we'll be moving out. We'll have a dress parade, too, and a message or a speech from a general. How do you feel about going off to fight, Charley?"

"I wish I was a real soldier, not just a drummer boy."

"Well, you'll be learning about war, anyhow. Don't expect to like it. You know what the soldiers say war is like."

"No, what?"

"It's four parts waiting, four parts blundering about, and three parts marching and fighting. Let me tell you a few things you ought to know."

"Sure, you tell us, Jem," came from a soldier lounging on a blanket a few feet away from Charley.

"You don't need to know, Jess. You were at Gettysburg," Jem retorted, then went on to Charley. "Well, Charley, some men see fighting one way. Some see it another. I'm a religious man. I think that every battle I come through is God's purpose for me. If He wants me to come through it, I will. Other men'll tell you each one of us has got a set time to die. That could be in a battle."

"Now, that ain't what I think, Jem," volunteered Jess, a thick-bodied man with heavy, dark brows. "I think every fight I come through makes it all the more likely I'll get killed or wounded in the next one."

This made Jem say, "I was about to get to that. That's what most soldiers think."

Charley asked, "Then if I'm going into my first fight, I ought to be all right, huh? Do Confederates fire at drummer boys?"

Jess grinned. "Bullets ain't particular about who they hit, kid. All the Johnny Rebs ain't sharpshooters. One of 'em could aim at the color-bearer of the 140th and hit somebody else."

"But ain't you supposed to pick out *one* enemy and aim at him?" asked Charley.

"That's what the officers tell us, but when the fightin' gets hot, you forget things. You jest flop down on your back, tear off cartridges with your teeth and reload your musket, roll over and shoot some more—even if it's only at smoke rollin' toward you—and hope you live through it."

"Jess, there's no call to scare the boy here!" As Jem put down the mended sock, he told Charley, "More soldiers in this man's Army die from sickness than battles. Bear that in mind. Thank God there ain't no malaria in Culpeper."

"But what do you think'll happen next, Jem?"

"We'll just sit here on our hunkers and wait and see."

While Charley Quinn fretted at the delay, Meade's great Army waited, going about its daily routine, until the first days of May came and the white-flowered dogwood trees bloomed.

On the first day of the month, the whole encampment knew they would soon be on the march. On the second, when the march order was actually given, an Ohio regiment mutinied, refusing to go, and General Meade threatened that any soldier who refused to do his duty would be shot without a trial.

Everyone, including Charley Quinn, knew that Meade and Grant intended to march out on the night of the third, with cavalry heading out first to the south and then the east. Behind the cavalry would come the marching men, cannon, and supply trains. They would cross the Rapidan River, pass as swiftly as possible through the Wilderness on its plank roads, and attack the Rebels on Lee's right flank before a full-scale battle began.

While they stood in the warm afternoon sunlight of the third, after a dress parade, General Meade reviewed them on his horse, Baldy. Later, he sent a brief message to be read to all the troops. Charley remembered one sentence particularly well and thought of Johnny as he heard it: "Bear with patience the hardships and sacrifices you will be called upon to endure. Keep your ranks on the battlefield. . . ." Oh, yes, his brother had done those things.

Later that day, Colonel Ayres of the 140th cried aloud to his assembled men from his horse, "We shall soon enough engage the enemy. Be cool. Keep ranks. Press forward, let the wounded lie where they are. Others will come for them. Aim low. Close steadily, then use your bayonets. Do not disgrace your state. If any man runs, I want those behind to shoot him. If they don't, I will."

As he heard these words, a thrill of pride in the 140th went through Charley Quinn's soul. A priest had come the night before to his regiment, said Mass for those who were Catholic, and heard confessions. Charley, his newly bestowed drum beside him, confessed his sin of running away from Noreen and received a penance of prayers. He was also given a rosary of his very own. The priest, a New Yorker, had known Johnny Quinn personally. He spoke highly to Charley of Johnny's courage. He went on to say that Charley could make his brother proud of him even though Johnny was no longer living.

How Charley wished he could write Noreen now that he was about to go into a fight! She'd replied to his letter saying she was relieved to learn where he was and that she hoped he'd take care of himself and keep safe from the Rebels. He hadn't replied to it yet.

The order to move out came that night. At an hour's notice, several thousand men and a great mass of equipment were to be on their way out of Culpeper— Charley Quinn, drummer boy of the 140th Veteran Volunteers, among them.

Silas knew the generals' plans—to pass through the Wilderness in one day's hard marching and give battle later in open country. The Army would leave in the night of May third and fourth with the cavalry leaving the camp first to act as scouts and skirmishers. If any Confederates out scouting were caught, the cavalry would deal with them. After the cavalry, the bridge-building engineers were to leave.

Silas came to Charley late that night to warn, "Charley, it's to be a long march—near to thirty miles, I hear. We got a river to cross, too. You'll be mighty tired at the end of all the walkin'."

Charley boasted, "Don't you worry about me. I can keep up. I may be tired, but I'll get there, too."

"Well, then, I won't worry. I'll see you later." Silas flashed a grin in the fading light of the camp fires and walked away, every inch the Union Army soldier.

Not long afterward, as the 140th stood ready and waiting, the order came from General Griffin to march out of camp to the Culpeper Road that led to Stevensburg.

Half running at times to keep up, Charley Quinn traveled beside the color-bearer of the 140th and some of the officers. Before long, the night march ceased to be an adventure to him as his drum, rations, and equipment began to weigh more and more. Yet, true to his promise to Silas, he kept going, putting one foot in front of the other.

On strict orders, the huge Army marched as silently as it could—men, wagons, riders, and even cattle driven along to supply fresh beef later on. When the first two army divisions came to the Rapidan River, they found that the engineers had done their work swiftly and surely. They had erected a bridge of floating canvas pontoons at Germanna Ford so the men could cross over on foot.

As Charley Quinn crossed over two abreast with an officer, he felt as if he were walking on jelly. The pontoons swayed so much that by the time he got onto the Germanna Plank Road below the bridge, he was dizzy, and the officer beside him had to grab him to steady him.

Soon they entered the twelve-by-fifteen-mile Wilderness, hated and feared by every man because all knew the misery it had caused during the lost Battle of Chancellorsville the previous year. All night the 140th and the many other regiments behind them marched along the narrow plank road. There was no singing the lilting "The Girl I Left Behind Me" now, as on the parade ground. There was no shouting of orders. When a courier galloped past, the sound of his horse's hooves was the only warning to make marching men give way. Charley was ever aware of the thick forest surrounding him. The memory of his first day out drumming with Silas haunted him. How glad he'd be to be out of here! Though there was to be no noise, there was some over the night cry of the whippoorwill. How could there be total silence with thousands of men on the move? Through the darkness came the sound of skillets clanking at men's belts, a sneeze or a cough, cursing as some sleepy infantryman fell against the man ahead of him, and always the soft shuffling of feet.

Around four in the morning, Charley grew so drowsy and weary that he started to stumble against the color-bearer. An officer nearby saw this, grabbed Charley by the arm and helped him along, then whispered an order to someone behind him, who went back at a run. Moments later, Captain Mahoney came up, trotting his horse to the front of the regiment. A long-armed soldier set Charley, drum and all, behind the captain, and from then on, the boy dozed with his arms around the captain's waist and his cheek on his back.

At noon, Charley's weary regiment caught up with Union Army cavalry at a tiny, middle-of-the-woods hamlet called Wilderness Tavern. As they rested here, a courier came galloping up to them from General Meade. The 140th and other infantry units were ordered to leave the horse soldiers, turn west, and march down another plank road called the Orange Turnpike. Here, a mile and a half west of Wilderness Tavern, they were to remain after they had flung a line of sentinels across that road.

Two hours later, Silas came over to Charley as he sat with his back to a tree beside his drum. "How are you?" Silas asked.

"All right. I got a ride partway here." Charley looked around him at the footsore men, sitting and lying on the ground beside the road. Then he looked at the closely spaced trees and said, "I want to get out of this place, though, Silas."

"You and me both. I hear we're more'n halfway out of the Wilderness. I don't want to look at another tree for a whole year after we get out of here."

"I wonder where the Rebels are."

"I dunno. Maybe they don't know where we are yet. I sure hope they don't. I hear tell we're supposed to stay here and hold this road for a while."

"How come we don't just rest a little and go on and get outa here?"

Gorman shook his head. "The generals make the rules, Charley. I learned a while back to rest every bit I can. Eat some of your rations. I don't think we'll be makin' any fires now. I have to get back. Maybe I'll come see you later on."

"Sure, Silas." Charley reached into his knapsack, took out some meat and hardtack, and chewed joylessly as he kept looking about. He sensed the trees—or something in them—watching him. He couldn't shake this feeling all day long.

As Charley slept that night in the dark camp, he dreamed near dawn of Johnny. In his dream the two of them fought against a howling throng of Dead Rabbits. He and Johnny were getting the worst of it.

7 THE BATTLE OF THE WILDERNESS

Charley awoke trembling at sunrise to find a hand on his shoulder, shaking him. Over the crackle of musket fire in the distance, a man's voice said into his ear, "Boy, get up and go to the colonel."

Charley got up, fastened on his drum, and hurried to where he'd seen his colonel lie down on a blanket like any other soldier. Something important was happening, for sure. Fallon was there with his bugle when he arrived.

Colonel Ayres, a medium-sized, handsome, bearded man, turned from his officers to the two boys. "The Confederates know we're here. That's skirmish fire you're hearing. They must have been just a few miles from us during the night. We're waiting to hear what orders General Griffin will give us."

Charley dared ask, "Will we be fighting here in the Wilderness, sir?"

"It appears so. Go out with your instruments and get the men up and ready. It doesn't matter how much noise you make now."

"Yes, sir," said Charley softly.

Together he and the bugler left the officers. Fallon blew reveille, and Charley beat out the signal Silas had shown him to assemble the men.

Things happened quickly after that. A rider came at a gallop down the Orange Turnpike to the 140th and the other units of the 1st Division. Griffin had ordered them to advance at seven-thirty with their entire force—to attack along the road.

By that hour, the whole division, thousands of men, was in full battle array. A moment after Charley heard the buglers of the various units sound the "advance," the 140th and all the others started forward down the turnpike and through the forest lining its sides, as they'd been ordered.

Then came what men feared most about this part of Virginia—getting lost. As soldiers moved forward, picking their way through the forest where twisting vines and thickets tore at their bodies and small trees grew so close to each other that it was impossible to squeeze through, their progress was slowed. Each part of the trackless Wilderness, though not far out of sight of the road, looked like every other part. Grimly, men walked onward, ever alert for the unseen enemy; but as they moved, they did lose sight of one another and their regiments.

Charley Quinn got lost with them, but by shouting and then by drumming his special signal, he finally was able to reassemble his scattered regiment in one spot. Pulling out Johnny's pocket watch, Charley saw that it was now late morning. They'd been lost for hours. He cursed the Wilderness.

When all of the lost regiments of the 1st Division eventually re-formed in the shelter of trees on the north side of the Orange Turnpike, two lines of attack were drawn up there. The 140th New York was on the left of the first long blue line, and behind them stood their old Gettysburg comrades, the 146th New York, nicknamed Garrard's Tigers.

At ten minutes to noon, Colonel Ayres gave Fallon and Charley the order to sound and beat the "charge." Charley drummed the long roll, a difficult signal that he had just mastered, and Fallon blew "forward." The hoarse cheer that roared up from the men thrilled Charley to the soles of his shoes. He cheered with them as they ran south out of their forest cover in a line of bright bayonets in the midday sunshine and into the trees across the turnpike. Sprinting beside the color-bearer, his heart beating as fast as his drum, Charley Quinn went forward with his regiment. As he ran and drummed, he whooped like an Indian or yelled "Hi-hee" along with the others around him.

Yankee cannon that had been brought down the Orange Turnpike from Culpeper sent shells screeching over their heads to smash into tree trunks, shattering them and sending limbs crashing down among the running men. Hundreds of sparrows fled shrieking from the mutilated trees. A red doe broke in alarm from her thicket and darted across the march of the 140th into a tall brake in one graceful, bounding motion.

Now unseen Rebel skirmishers, sharpshooters sent out ahead of their regiments, commenced to fire on the advancing bluecoats. The crackle of rifles was suddenly all around Charley as he beat his drum with fingers slick with sweat. He saw men throw up their arms and fall on either side of him as he ran to keep pace with the color-bearer. He stared down at the fallen soldiers in horror, but his drumbeat drove him on as it did the others. Not realizing what he did, he moved along like the others, head downward, leaning forward as against a strong wind.

At Sanders Field, a clearing with a gully in it, the advancing boy caught sight of his first Johnny Rebs, men not in gray as he had expected but in butternut brown. They were running away, looking over their shoulders as they fled down the gully and up over the slope onto the other side. The 140th came after them without a pause. Charley heard Colonel Ayres shouting, "Steady. Steady, men, steady," and Charley came along steadily, his blood drumming in his ears and his thoughts disconnected and fleeting—of Noreen and her sewing machine, of Broadway's traffic which he dodged so nimbly, of the Dead Rabbit he had fought.

The 140th soon learned why the Rebels had given up the fight and fled so easily before them. It had been a trap! Hundreds of Confederates lay at the top of the gully behind felled trees made into breastworks. Down in the gully, Charley Quinn's regiment drew a hideous cross fire from Rebel-filled stands of timber in front of them and to the right.

Driven in on itself, the 140th crowded to the left back toward the Orange Turnpike road. Charley went with them, keeping close to his colonel. As he stood next to the officer, drumming the long roll steadily, a Rebel minié ball—a small, round, hollow musket shell—

whistled past his left elbow and smashed into the head of his drum. No sound could come from it now. Charley stood motionless, staring at it, his drumsticks lifted.

Then, all at once, a hoarse shout, "Hurrah, boys. Hurrah!" attracted his attention. To his right he saw Jem Miller, shouting for all he was worth, his legs pumping toward the Confederates' logs. The boy looked on in horror as Jem dropped his musket, spread wide his arms, and crumpled onto the ground at the bottom of the gully. Jem? Jem dead? Dead in the early-afternoon light of such a warm spring day? It could not be. In Charley's brain something howled, "No!"

Charley ran to his fallen friend. A quick glance showed him the red hole in his forehead, the mark of a sharpshooter. In a flash, Charley had Jem's musket to his shoulder. The man had been a careful soldier. He'd have a fresh charge in it if he was running to meet the enemy. Taking aim, little Charley Quinn chose his man, a lanky, brown-bearded Confederate standing atop the logs looking for a target for his own musket. Charley fired. The Rebel dropped his gun and clutched at his shoulder. Blood began to well between his fingers, and he fell backward over the breastworks.

Now the truth flooded Charley's consciousness. Gone were thoughts of heroism and revenge. He had shot a man! He was only twelve years old, and he'd shot and killed a human being. What should he do now? He didn't know. He cried out wordlessly, threw down Jem's musket, and with the useless drum banging at his hip, sprinted for the wooded clearing to the left. Musket balls speeding toward him hummed beelike and tore away fragments of cloth from his sleeve and trousers.

As he ran, he spied Silas Gorman lying sprawled not thirty feet away. He could see him clearly through drifting curls of smoke. Silas had torn away the seams of one leg of his trousers and was staring down at a bloody wound on his shin. He saw Charley and beckoned to him, his mouth open in a call for help that could not be heard over the shouting, screaming, crackling, and booming that filled the gully. Silas wanted him! Silas needed him!

But Charley Quinn did not break his stride to go to his friend. He ran on among the dead and wounded, racing faster, stumbling forward.

Something strange had happened to his vision. Everything he saw was crystal-clear—fluffy white smoke drifting over the clearing from all the firing going on, falling leaves clipped by musket balls, the open red mouths of the yelling, charging men of the 140th—and the startled eyes of Con Sullivan as he saw Charley fleeing.

As the boy ran by him, he heard Con's voice bellowing, "Charley, skedaddle! Go on. Run away. Run, ye coward Bowery bummer!"

An officer picked up Sullivan's cry. "Run, run, ye damned whelp. Run home to your mama!" he shouted, and lifted his pistol to shoot at Charley but did not pull the trigger.

Running toward the end of the bluecoat troops, Charley spotted Dan Whaley, the Dead Rabbit who had recognized him that first day in Culpeper. He didn't shout at him but watched as Charley streaked past. Other men who knew him as the regimental drummer boy saw and marked him with their eyes. An officer at the rear swatted at him with the flat of his sword to drive him back and missed.

Charley Quinn kept on running to the left even when he'd passed by all of the men of the 140th New York. He ran like a fear-crazed animal up over the rim of the gully until a clump of roots lying in his path brought him down to a crashing halt flat on his face.

There he lay for a little while panting for breath. The sound of firing and yelling behind him came clearly to his ears. He got up, detached the useless drum from its sash, and dropped both it and the sash onto the earth. The drumsticks were behind him where he'd dropped them at the clearing. He lurched over to the little creek coming out of a swamp, the creek he'd passed, drumming proudly, just a few minutes before. He bent down to cup water to soothe his burning face. Then he got up, waded across the water, and followed the swamp quite a distance to a particularly dense thicket of undergrowth.

Crawling inside it, Charley sat, with his head on his drawn-up knees, listening to the battle, trying to pray, sobbing in the shame and misery of his desertion. In his mind, he saw Johnny's and Jem's and Silas's accusing faces. He could hear Con's well-remembered voice taunting him. As the boy sat there, a terrorized rabbit came leaping into the thicket to snuggle wild-eyed up against his arm. Charley looked at its quivering sides and trembling whiskers. The battle had made a runaway, a skedaddler, out of it, too, but it was only a rabbit, not a soldier. A rabbit could be expected to run—but not

Charley Quinn. That skedaddler had killed a man and then had turned and run—and everybody knew it.

Deep sobs racked Charley's body. He threw himself full-length onto the earth, pounding it, startling the rabbit that had sought refuge by him, making it pin back its ears and lope away. He'd failed this poor frightened creature, too. Charley sat up again, folded his arms on his knees, and lay his head on the blue cloth he was not fit to wear.

8 THE REBS

The night was quiet, but not the dawn of the sixth of May. The crackling of musket fire came to Charley's ears on all sides. More fighting. Not knowing what else to do, he stayed where he was until a new fear propelled him into action. Fire! Fires from the sparks of thousands of cannon shells had sprung up among the dry leaves of the Wilderness and roared over acres of timberland. Now the gray smoke billowing from them, mixing with gunpowder fumes, drove Charley Quinn out of his protective thicket.

Coughing, frightened by the smoke, he bent to wet his pocket handkerchief in swamp water and tie it around his nose and mouth. As he stooped at the edge of the stinking dark water, he heard a sharp clicking sound he recognized. The cocking of a pistol. Straightening and whirling around, Charley looked up into the face of a lantern-jawed, sallow, yellow-haired man in a brown-yellow short jacket, blue Union army trousers, and a gray forage cap. A Rebel, for sure! In his hand was a huge, long-barreled cavalry pistol. It was aimed at Charley's head. The boy froze.

First the man shot a wad of tobacco juice at Charley's feet, then he asked softly, "What've we got here? I'd say it was a redhead Yankee boy. Kinda small, ain'tcha? If you were a turtle now, I'd throw you back in the swamp to grow up some. Who'd you be?"

Charley faltered. "I was a drummer boy. My name's Charley." After that he fell silent.

"Charley what?"

"Make it Skedaddle," Charley told him bitterly.

The Confederate laughed. "That's some queer old name you got. Come along with me, boy. My officer'll want to talk to you. Give me your knapsack and jest move out ahead of me."

"Who are you?" Charley asked.

"Who I am don't matter."

Was he a prisoner? Charley sank his teeth into his lower lip to keep from crying. What would happen to him now? What did the Johnny Rebs do with Yankee drummer boy prisoners?

Charley tied the wet cloth over his face and, hands in the air, began to walk ahead of his Rebel captor. It was hard going through the tangle of vines and hickory bushes that tore at his uniform. Twice he fell and was prodded to his feet by the toe of his captor's boot and the words, "Git on up, Yankee boy. I ain't got all day to fetch you back to where we got to go."

Deep among the thickets and trees, Charley could not see fifteen feet ahead of him, but on either side he saw clearly the dead bodies of men dressed in blue and butternut-brown and gray uniforms lying stiff and staring. Sometimes tongues of flame shot up so near that their clothing was singed. The brush hissed and popped in the heat as bright red sparks flew over their heads. Surely this was like the hell the sisters in school and the priest in church had warned him about.

After much turning and twisting, they arrived at a clearing filled with men dressed in the butternut-brown color of the Confederate Army. A half dozen bluecoat soldiers sat on the ground with their hands folded on top of their heads.

Charley's captor told him, "Git on over there and sit down with them other bluebellies."

The boy did as he was told. Looking from face to face, he was relieved to see no one he knew. He took the handful of skillet-parched corn a Reb gave him and tried to chew it. He couldn't and had to spit it out. Rebel soldiers watching him laughed. One said, "It's what we got to eat. Ain't it good enough for you, Yankee brat?"

A Rebel officer in a very tattered, soiled gray coat came over to the prisoners to warn, "Don't you Union men do any talking to one another. I'll personally shoot the man who does. Someone'll be coming to get you soon."

His words proved true. Very shortly three Confederate soldiers with muskets and shining bayonets came to roust the Yankees up and send them walking ahead of them.

An hour's marching of nearly three miles brought Charley and the others through the Wilderness to a large open space where they once again were told to sit. There was a farmhouse, a barn, and some other outbuildings here, as well as hundreds of shabbily dressed Confederate soldiers. Most were gaunt and grimy. Not a few were shoeless. Some wore gray forage caps; others wore brown slouch hats over a mixture of gray and butternut-brown jackets and coats. Some had on Union-blue trousers stripped from the enemy dead.

White smoke from the muskets firing among the trees mingled with the darker smoke from the Wilderness fires. Coming across the open space in acrid-smelling wreaths, it made men cough and sneeze. Charley put the handkerchief up over his nose and mouth again.

The boy was just settling himself onto the ground when he was forced to leap to his feet to keep from being run over by a host of men racing toward him. Rebels! Rebels retreating as fast as they could.

Then a great animal-like roar rose up from a thousand throats, and Charley saw other tattered Rebels racing forward through the ranks of their retreating comrades. A charge! As they ran, they screeched the famous Rebel yell, *"Ee ee-ee-ee-ee."*

Behind them came a tall, gray-bearded officer in a gray uniform under a black cloak, riding a dapple-gray horse with a black mane and tail. As the officer reached the charging men, a few of them, hearing the hoofbeats, slackened their speed. At once, a wild shouting rose up from these men: "Go back, General Lee. Go back!"

Lee? Robert E. Lee? Charley Quinn gaped in amazement, as did the other prisoners. Generals were seldom seen anywhere, and certainly not in infantry charges.

Charley watched, fascinated, as a sergeant of the charging Texas Brigade sprang forward to grab hold of the bridle of Lee's horse, stopping the famous Traveller from going into battle with his master.

Now many Texans halted their attack to turn and shout, "We won't go unless you go back!"

A Confederate officer rode up to Lee's side and began to argue with him. When Lee slowly shook his head, the sergeant let go of the rein to release it to his commander-in-chief. An enormous cheer crashed into the smoky air as Robert E. Lee turned his horse around and began to ride toward some horsemen in a knoll to his right.

"Lee! Lee!" echoed soldiers' deep voices. While their comrades cheered, those men of the Texas Brigade who had forced Lee back to safety resumed their charge against the Yankees among the trees.

As for Charley Quinn, he sat down again at a bayonet's prod until a corporal came over, pointed to him, and then jerked him to his feet. Hustled along, he was taken to a tent where a sad-faced, balding Confederate officer sat at a little folding table. It was hot inside, and the front and rear tent flaps were open for ventilation.

Once the corporal had gone, the officer asked, "Who are you, lad?"

"Charley. Charley Skedaddle."

"I know that word. And I doubt that is your real last name."

Charley swallowed and said, "It's Quinn, sir."

"You are not a soldier, are you?"

"No, sir. I never signed any papers to enlist. I was only a drummer."

At this, the officer put down the pen he had in his hand. "A drummer boy. I thought as much. What is your age?"

"Twelve, sir."

"What is your regiment?"

Charley didn't answer. All soldiers had been warned that if they were ever captured, they were to tell only their name and rank. He had done that already, and now he said, "I can't tell you that, sir."

The officer smiled slightly. "Have you ever gone to school?"

"Oh, yes, sir. I can read and write just dandy."

"I'm glad to hear it. I was a schoolmaster at one time." He sighed. "How did you get separated from your regiment? I think you can tell me *that*, you know."

Blushing, Charley lowered his gaze. He stuttered, "I— I got scared when I saw my drum hit by a minié ball and saw my friend Jem get killed, so I ran away." Mother Mary, no, he wouldn't dare say he'd picked up a musket and killed a Reb. That'd bring him more trouble, for sure.

"So you ran away? I thought you had. Well, you are only a child, after all. Have you ever heard of Andersonville Prison?"

"No, sir, I haven't."

The Confederate officer sighed again. "It's a prison camp for Yankee soldiers down in Georgia. It would be a very bad place to send a boy your age. You should be in a classroom. If any of the men from your regiment in Andersonville found out you were a deserter, it would be even worse for you. Well, then, I think I shall have to do something else with you. You will note that I have not written down one word about you. I'll have no record of you."

"What will you do with me, sir?"

"Have you any money with you?"

"A little bit."

"Good. Yankee money is worth quite a bit more here than our money. Do you see the open tent flap behind me?"

"Yes, sir, I do."

"Then be so good, Charley Skedaddle, as to skedaddle through it right now. As I see it, you are of no use to us. And I don't want it on my conscience that I sent a twelve-year-old boy to Andersonville."

"You're letting me go?"

"Yes, I am. There is a thicket of some size behind this tent. Get into it and stay there until this battle is over and we move on."

"But where'll I go after that, sir?"

"That is up to you." The officer frowned. "If you go north, you'll run into your own troops. If you go south, you'll be captured again and may fare differently with some other man. If you go east, you could run into battle after battle. That's where the fighting is going to be next, unless I miss my guess. What's left to you, then?"

"The west!" said Charley, unable to believe his good fortune.

"Then west it has to be. That's mountain country here in Virginia. You will find it very different from New York City, but I see it as your only refuge right now."

Charley gasped out, "How did you know I was from New York City?"

"Your manner of speaking and how you pronounce words. I've been there. I've made a study of accents. That's why I was given this particular chore with prisoners who will not talk. Get rid of your uniform if you know what is good for you. Now, my boy, do as I tell you. Skedaddle before I change my mind. I don't fancy deserters—no matter how young they may be."

"Thank you, thank you, sir." After lifting his hat, Charley Quinn shot like a bolt past the man's table and out the rear flap of the tent. He sprinted for the nearby hickory thicket and dived inside, all the while thanking the guardian angel the sisters said he always had with him for his deliverance. Once inside the thicket, he took off his blue uniform blouse, discarded his cap, and began to pick at the stripe sewn along the sides of his trousers as part of his splendid drummer boy's uniform.

Lying on his belly in the thicket on that long, hot day, Charley had a lot of time to think and wonder, and the heat of shame crept up to his cheeks as he thought of Silas and Jem. They had not run! They'd fought it out. Had Silas died, too? What had happened to the 140th? Where were they now? Still fighting here in the Wilderness? Were most of them dead, as his friends were?

Would Noreen get a letter from someone in the 140th telling her that he had run away, or would whoever wrote her be kind enough to say he was "missing in action," perhaps even mention that he had picked up a musket and used it?

Used a musket? Yes. Each time he closed his eyes, Charley could again see the man he'd shot and killed.

Mother Mary! He'd committed a mortal sin. He wasn't a real soldier who had orders to do that to an enemy. Where could he confess his sin? Where could he find a priest? He should have gone back to the rear of his regiment and halted there, ready to be captured; or else he should have tried to get a new drum from the supply wagon. If he'd done that, he wouldn't be caught in this nightmare now.

But he hadn't. He'd killed a man, and then he'd run and kept on running. Now look at him—he was no longer in any uniform at all. And he was alone and nameless in a thicket somewhere in the dreaded Wilderness.

The fight went on and on till sunset, and while it did, Charley lay in his thicket, afraid to move lest he be discovered. Insects crawled over him, and once a brown-bodied little snake twisted by, not three feet from his motionless hand. Oh, how did he ever find himself in this vile, hellish place? Why did he ever leave the Bowery? Sweet Mother of God, how he missed New York! How he wished he were back in the Bowery among his friends. He'd give anything to be with Noreen. He'd even be glad to see Mr. Demarest. They would find him different now—they would. He would even give up his membership in the Bowery Boys if Noreen wanted.

Dozens of thoughts and recriminations, all of them sad or frightening, went through Charley's head as he lay there, until finally, worn out by anguish, fear, and hunger, he fell asleep, his face pressed to the red soil. And while he slept, the Battle of the Wilderness slowed and then petered out in the darkness.

9 BOY ALONE!

As long as he dared, Charley waited in his thicket the next morning—waited, tormented by smoke, until he saw the red of flames through stalks nearby. There was no safety for him here any longer. He crawled out of his refuge, leaving behind the clothing that would mark him as being from the Yankee Army.

Once away from the shelter, the boy looked about him fearfully. The tent of the Confederate officer who had questioned him was gone. The Rebs had marched away. The clearing where he'd seen General Lee on horseback was almost empty now, save for a dozen or so men in butternut brown who were occupied with a grisly task. Bodies of the Rebel dead lay in a row on the trampled earth where they'd been dragged from the forest. As Charley looked on from behind a tree, he saw two of the soldiers lift a corpse by its feet and arms and put it into a waiting wagon filled with other corpses. Charley swallowed hard and backed away.

What should he do? Where was he, anyhow? The

officer had said he should go to the west. But which way was west from here? Barely visible above the smoke-filtering handkerchief tied about his face, Charley's forehead creased with thought. He'd marched with the 140th down the Germanna Plank Road, which he knew ran north and south. Then he'd turned at Wilderness Tavern onto another road, the Orange Turnpike. It had run in another direction from the Germanna road, so it had to run east to west. The Johnny Reb who had captured him must have taken him south to join up with the Confederate troops coming north from the town of Orange. It seemed to Charley that he must somehow find the Orange Turnpike again. But how could he do that? There was only one answer—head in the direction from which the Texas Brigade had been attacking yesterday. But how to do that without being seen and recaptured? And what if he got lost again as he had before with his regiment? Lost alone in the Wilderness? Mother Mary, no!

Charley looked behind him. No one was looking toward him. If he moved swiftly and quietly and took advantage of the foul-scented smoke wafting over the clearing, he might be able to make it into the forest unnoticed. Yes, he'd go. He'd risk it! He had no other choice.

Bending low, Charley ran forward. Sheltering behind every tree, every bit of undergrowth and drift of smoke, he made it unseen to the thickset trees that fringed the clearing. In a moment, he was among them, moving as fast as he could away from the clearing. Once in the trees, he sat down to catch his breath. Now, which direction should he take? He wanted to go north to find the turnpike road, but what would he find there if he did—the Union Army?

More important, though, which way was north? Charley thought of something now that had not seemed important at the time. Sister Mary Michael had once told his class something a long time ago when they were studying botany. She said that moss grew on the north side of trees. If she said so, it had to be true.

Charley got up and began to hunt for moss on the young trees around him. It took a bit of searching, but in time he found one with moss on its trunk. Beyond it lay two others.

Charley made his way, tree by tree, ever deeper into the smoky Wilderness. He avoided fires and bypassed swamps and waded the creeks, always moving as silently and stealthily as he could. Sometimes he saw men in gray and butternut brown moving in the smoky distance, and then he froze, hiding in the brush until they had gone on, seeking bodies.

He saw dead men, too, a pair of Confederates and a few Union soldiers, sometimes lying close together like slumbering comrades, sometimes far apart. A Yankee sergeant lay facedown, as if clutching the earth. A Johnny Reb, equally stiff in death, lay on his back, looking with surprise up at the trees, where smoke mingled with the blue skies. One soldier in butternut brown lay half in, half out of an oozing swamp creek. Charley shuddered.

He needed water, but he dared not fill his nearly empty canteen here in the Wilderness. He knew what he must do. Gritting his teeth, fighting nausea, Charley went to each of the dead soldiers in turn, hunting for the man's canteen. Two had no canteens with them. Other thirsty men had taken them before Charley Quinn came. Another had a little left in his, and that of the fourth soldier was bone-dry. The Yankee who lay facedown had his canteen under his body.

To get it, Charley had to use the knife he'd brought from the Bowery to cut the leather strap that held it. Pulling on one end of the strap, he still couldn't get the canteen loose. At last, with tears of horror brimming his eyes, Charley set his feet against the man's heavy body and jerked with all his might. The bloodstained canteen came free with a rush that bowled the boy over onto his back. Charley scrambled to his feet, shaking all over.

He jiggled the canteen to hear its sound. It was half full. Charley stayed near the dead soldier long enough to whisper to him, "I'm sorry. I have to have it, though. Thank you." Then he ran to a tree broader than the others, giving him more cover, and, behind it, poured the contents of the sergeant's brown-stained canteen into his own. For the first time that day, Charley drank and then used a little liquid to moisten his handkerchief. A moment later, steeling himself again, he went back to the Yankee to hunt in the man's haversack for food. All he could find was hardtack, and he took that, broke it into fragments, and put it into his pockets.

Munching crumbs of the biscuit, Charley started out again, striking north.

In the distance, he saw other men moving now, bluecoat ones. They, too, were looking for bodies. Charley avoided them with the care he'd used with the Johnny Rebs. Once somebody hailed him with a shout.

Charley didn't reply. He slid under a fallen log, sharing the space with a host of crawling beetles, till he figured the man had given up and gone about his business. Then he started out once more.

Several hours of walking brought him at last to the Orange Turnpike. Charley stumbled out of a dense growth of trees, and there it was in front of him—the road that two days before had swarmed with foot soldiers and echoed to the hoofbeats of cavalry. It was now smoky but deserted. There certainly must have been fighting on this stretch of road. Treetops were shorn off—the sign of cannon fire—and the edge of the road was trampled on both sides, showing that wagons and cavalry had passed along it. But there was nobody now, nothing living, save two hawks making great circles in the hot blue sky.

West! The officer had said to go west, so Charley walked out onto the turnpike and started warily down it, his eyes searching ahead and behind, his ears always alert to the slightest sound.

In mid-afternoon he heard the sound of a horse's hooves. An army courier? No, messengers rode at a gallop, and this was a slow clopping of hooves, with the creaking of wheels audible above it.

Charley left the turnpike for the shelter of trees and, knowing himself to be screened from view, waited. Soon he saw an old wagon and a bony sorrel horse approaching in the smoky distance. The wagon was driven by an ancient black man in a long, dark coat and shapeless, light yellow hat. This was no army wagon, to say the least.

Remembering big Marcus back in Culpeper, Charley was not afraid. He pulled down his handkerchief, left his hiding place, and ran down onto the road waving his arms. Startled, the black man reined in his horse. He looked on in surprise as Charley came running to him.

"Are you going to the west, too?" Charley asked him.

The old man didn't speak. He only stared as the boy repeated his question. Then Charley pointed to the west. Perhaps the old man was deaf. Charley pointed again, nodded, then pointed to himself.

At that moment, there came a dull booming sound in the far distance: cannon fire. The fighting was still going on somewhere. Both Charley and the old man jumped at the sudden noise. So he wasn't deaf, thought Charley.

When the booming ceased, the old driver nodded. He said, "Ah'm headed near to the mountains."

Charley asked, "Will you give me a ride? I'll pay you if you'll take me."

Once more the black man stared, then he grinned and nodded again. Next he patted the place on the seat next to him.

"That's right," Charley exclaimed. "I want a ride." And he climbed up over the wheel into the wagon seat.

After thanking his benefactor, the boy introduced himself and told the man that he came from New York City. The old man was a dandy listener. He never once interrupted, and he appeared to listen closely. He'd look intensely at Charley who, because he felt encouraged, talked on and on about the Bowery Boys and Broadway and Johnny and Noreen—about everything except the battle he'd run from and the Union Army.

By late afternoon, Charley was talked out, and the old black man had yet to say another word, though he had continued to look often and questioningly at the boy. So they creaked along in silence through countryside that seemed almost drained of life. Ahead of the wagon, growing ever nearer, rose the Blue Ridge Mountains, a barrier Charley knew he must cross to get to the west.

At sunset, a wild black and gold and red one because of the smoke, the old man pulled his horse to a halt where a narrow road bisected the turnpike. He turned to Charley, pointed to the narrow road, and said, "Ah goes down here now."

Charley nodded. He'd have to walk again. Well, he was grateful for the ride. He reached into his pocket and gave the old man fifteen cents, which he figured he owed him. The old black man took only a five-cent piece and handed the rest back to the boy.

Though he didn't want to take it, Charley did. He might need it. He had ten dollars and twenty cents. Although he'd been paid his thirteen dollars the first of the month, he'd bought peppermints and a three-dollar harmonica in Culpeper. It had fallen out of his pocket somewhere in his wild dash away from the battle.

Getting down, Charley stood at the sorrel's bridle and said, "Thank you. It was sure nice of you to take me along with you."

He waited for the man to say something. At last he did. First, he shook his head, and slowly he said, "Boy, ah never did understand hardly one word you was sayin' to me. I listened hard, too. Where in the world do you come from where folks talk like you do?"

Leaving Charley openmouthed with astonishment, the old man clucked to his horse and reined it to the left leaving the main road. Staring after him, Charley told himself that he had clearly told the man he hailed from

New York City. He was thunderstruck to think that his accent couldn't be understood by everyone. Charley sighed. If this was the way it was down here, what would it be like in the mountains?

Now that he was alone again, Charley felt the bad memories of the day before crowding in on him again. His shoulders drooped as he started off on foot to where the mountains were jutting blackly against the sky. What he needed now was a place to sleep in safety for the night.

Just before dark, he spied a house—a cabin, really— down a road that ran to the right. It had not been burned as so many houses had, and it looked deserted. Charley scouted the cabin carefully, circling it, but no one came out. Finally, he opened the front door and went inside. Knife in hand, he searched the place. It was abandoned and held nothing in the way of furnishings at all.

Charley chose his sleeping place with care. He lay down on the floor near the back door, ready to leap up and run out the rear if anyone came to the house.

He was learning what he had already guessed—that the life of a deserter here in Virginia wasn't going to be an easy one. Once he'd crossed the mountains out of this state and was away from the war, he ought to be able to breathe easier and find a place where the fighting wasn't apt to come, a place where nobody would ever suspect he was a skedaddling Union Army drummer boy. There he would call himself Charley Quinn again.

As he curled up to sleep, he told himself that tomorrow he'd have to start climbing. He would need tonight's rest. He hoped he wouldn't dream of the dead Confederate he'd shot or relive the battle as he had the last two nights.

10 JERUSHA

Mockingbirds quarreling noisily with other birds awakened Charley at daybreak from a restless sleep. For a time, he was able to put the memory of his disgrace behind him by making plans for his future. He'd go over the mountains and stay there for a while. Then he'd head for the north someplace where nobody knew him. After a long time, when he was grown up to be a man and no one would recognize him, he'd come back to New York on a visit to Noreen. Yes, he'd grow himself a mustache like Johnny had. That should change his looks a lot—that and growing taller, too.

Well, in the meantime, he might as well eat some hardtack and have a swig of water and be on his way.

Although the Blue Ridge Mountains looked close by to Charley as he walked along the turnpike road, he soon learned the deceptiveness of distance. Though he walked and walked, they grew nearer only after many miles of effort.

He saw few people in the hamlets he went through. It

was as if the people hid from him as he walked past the frame and redbrick houses and stores. Dogs barked and followed him for a while and then were whistled back by someone unseen. Used to the clamor of the city he knew so well and to Culpeper camp, Charley found this eerie. He saw curtains twitch as he passed, so there were people. Why were they wary of a solitary boy?

Around mid-morning, Charley heard the jingling noise of harnesses and the thudding of hoofbeats from behind him. He hurriedly left the road for the safety of a ditch a few yards from it. Cavalry! As he peered from behind tall, swaying wildflowers, he saw a troop of graycoat horsemen pass by at a steady trot. Johnny Rebs out scouting! Charley heard their leader call a halt just opposite him and talk to some of the troopers behind him. They stopped for a while with the commander, who finally swung his horse about and stared back at the road. Then they all turned their mounts and headed back at the same gait at which they had come. Charley waited to scramble out of his ditch until they were gone from view, clanking and jingling, around a bend in the road.

It was noon when he finally reached the foothills of the mountains. Here the road began to rise. Putting one foot heavily in front of the other, Charley climbed. This part of Virginia was different from Culpeper and the Wilderness. It, too, was wooded, but here the forests were different. Trees he didn't begin to know the names of were massed together under a strange blue haze. Among them were dense thickets of a gray-green laurel, and among the thickets stood beautiful mountain dogwood trees, some still dotted with white blossoms. Here up high, the cool air was tangy with the scent of pine, and there was no trace of the foul smoke of the Wilderness fires at all.

As he climbed in the late afternoon, Charley felt the mountains around him. They weren't like the Wilderness, filled with evil smells and memories, but all the same, they were frightening. Their enormous forested bulk, towering over the road on both sides of him as well as ahead and behind, made him feel hemmed in. He sensed that the trees watched him. There was no friendliness coming from them as he'd felt from the trees in Central Park. Here was a waiting, brooding atmosphere. Although he had neither passed nor seen anyone since he began to climb, he felt eyes boring into his back. Whenever he turned his head quickly to look about, he expected to see someone, but he never did. What kinds of wild animals lived up here? He heard noises from the sides of the road at times, but he saw nothing.

And then suddenly, as he stopped to rest for a bit, he heard the blast of a horn from somewhere above him. What could this mean? Charley froze.

Some moments afterward, a young man in a big black hat and tattered gray coat came pelting down the road toward him. As he ran past Charley, he called out, "The conscriptors have come agin. Hide yerself." And the man ran on and darted into laurels on the right side of the road.

Conscriptors? What were they? Whatever they were, they had to be dangerous to make somebody so scared. Taking a hint from the ragged man, Charley plunged into high, thick-growing rhododendrons on the left, crouched down, and waited.

Before long, he saw a group of six Confederate soldiers come along the road, one on horseback, four walking. The sixth man, a bearded blond giant, walked, too, but with his arms bound behind his back. He was scowling as he passed by Charley's hiding place going back downhill along the road—back toward the war. Who could he be? He was wearing a gray jacket and butternut-brown trousers. Suddenly, Charley thought he knew who he was—a Johnny Reb deserter caught here in the mountains. Had the tattered man been a deserter, too? Whoever he was, Charley Quinn didn't want to meet him again.

Once the six men passed, Charley worked his way through the rhododendrons. He noticed that there was a path behind the plants and followed it, figuring it would go back to the road he had just left. It didn't. It climbed and twisted and turned along ridges with ever-deepening ravines and narrow meadows covered with bluish grass.

By sunset, Charley had no idea where he was. According to the trees he examined for moss, he was going north. So to find the road again, he would have to retrace his steps. But not this day. He couldn't risk falling down a ravine in the darkness.

And then all at once, he saw a little cluster of buildings nestled under tall evergreens in a clearing. The buildings, only vague gray shapes in the hazy dusk, were set behind a low, sagging fence. There were only four of them, two large and the others very small. A farm, more than likely. He'd seen farms around Culpeper, so he knew one when he saw it. The bigger building with the stone chimney and the corncrib attached would be the dwelling place, and the other big one the shed. The smaller ones could be henhouses. A henhouse! Eggs!

He liked eggs. Noreen had made omelets once when he'd brought home fresh eggs from a street peddler.

But how could he get them? He didn't want to go to the door and ask to buy food. Who knew what sort of welcome a Yankee deserter would get? He decided instead to sneak into the henhouse, take the eggs he found, and leave a penny payment in each nest. He'd get away as fast as he could, sleep where he felt it would be safest, and by daybreak be going back down the path to the main road.

What he had to do right now was wait till it was full dark, then he'd circle around the house to the woods behind it and work up unseen to the henhouse. But was there a dog around?

He had to find that out. But how? Silas would have known. A hot flood of shame came over Charley at this thought of his friend. Oh, Silas! Shaking off his feeling of guilt, Charley picked up a small stone at his feet and hurled it against the shed. As he heard it hit, he flung himself full-length into the tall grass and waited. No dog barked. Nothing at all happened except that the front door of the house opened for an instant, then swiftly closed. No one called out, but now a light showed in the window that had been dark before. Somebody lived here, but at least there was no dog to reckon with.

As Charley waited for darkness, he took the last fragments of hardtack from his pocket and ate them, licking the crumbs from the palm of his hand. Then he got to his feet and ran for the fence, put both hands on it, and vaulted over. It was so old and ill kept that it almost collapsed under him. He'd have to go over it more carefully with the fragile eggs. He worked his way as silently as possible around to the side of the house where the coop was located.

Stepping gingerly over the soft earth, he reached the coop and was about to lift its latch when all of a sudden he heard a ferocious hissing, followed by a loud honking and the rustling clatter of wings. A moment later, a door opened nearby, and his eyes were struck by the yellow light of a lantern.

Over the honking and hissing, a harsh voice rang out, "Stand where ya are, Boy, or I'll shoot ya."

Shoot? Charley's hand fell at once from the latch. He cried out, "I only came for eggs. I was going to pay for them."

"Ha!" The laughter was as harsh as the voice. Then whoever it was commanded, "Stop that thar ruction, Malindy. Ya, Boy, don't move at all."

Charley stood motionless while the kerosene lantern was set down on a bench on the back porch of the cabin. Silhouetted in front of its light were the black figures of a large goose and a tall person, in a shirt and trousers, who held the longest pistol Charley had ever seen. An old flintlock, it was larger than cavalrymen carried. Who was his captor this time?

"Who'd ya be?" demanded the voice.

"C-Charley," Charley stammered.

"Charley what?"

"Charley Skedaddle."

This made the person laugh. "Skedaddle's a good name for the likes of ya. I never seen ya before, and I know jest about ever'body hereabouts. So ya must come from down yonder. Do ya be an outlander, Boy?"

"Yes, sir, I guess I am."

"Why'd ya come here?"

"To get some eggs. I'm hungry."

"Why didn' ya 'hello' the house and ask me for 'em?"

Charley hung his head. What should he say now? He was a Union Army deserter in the mountains of a Confederate state.

"Why not ask me for 'em?" his captor repeated. "Are ya a soldier?"

"No." Charley shook his head.

"Yes, ya be too small for that. Ya talk queer, I'd say. Ya ain't from Virginia. Where do ya come from?"

Charley sighed. "New York City, mister."

"I ain't no mister. My name's Jerusha Bent."

"Jerusha?" Charley had never heard the name before.

"In these parts, that's a name for womenfolks. I'm Granny Jerusha Bent. A man'd be called Jerusalem."

Charley goggled at her. A woman in britches! Yet with such a Bible-sounding name, there ought to be hope. He asked, figuring the big woman would be generous, "Will you let me have some eggs if I give you a penny each for them?"

Again the laugh. "That's a mighty handsome price, but they ain't for sale." Then, to Charley's huge relief, the long pistol was set on the bench beside the lantern. Now the tall woman said, "I figger ya to be a deserter from the Yankee Army. I been thinkin' on where ya say ya come from. I heard it said New York was way up in the north. Are ya from the Yankee Army that's down in the bluegrass country now?"

Charley sighed in his unhappiness. "Yes."

"A deserter, then?"

"Yes."

"Ya ran away from a fight?"

Charley nodded. To his surprise, the woman didn't show disgust. But then, maybe she was used to deserters. Perhaps there were other Union Army deserters here in these mountains, men he could join up with. His hopes rose.

"Are there other men like me here, Miss Bent?"

"It's jest Granny Bent, and no, there ain't no men like ya here. What lets ya call yerself a man, a runty boy like ya are? These hills are for the South. Yankee deserters who get kotched here don' live to tell it. I oughta shoot ya down where ya are."

Charley tensed himself to run, but Granny Bent didn't reach for her pistol. Instead she folded her arms and said, "Come closer. Don' ya be scared. I don' aim to shoot ya."

Slowly, Charley stepped forward to the edge of the porch. From there, he said, "I saw Reb deserters here today. I don't suppose you'd shoot one of them."

The woman sniffed. "If he come here after my eggs, I would." She bent over to pat the goose's sleek head. "Malindy would let me know if anybody came too close—like she did with ya. Better'n any hound, that's my Malindy. There are Confederate deserters here-abouts, but most of 'em came from here in the fust place. They got weary of the war an' come home. Their folks hide 'em."

"They're lucky," said Charley bitterly.

"How old are ya?"

"I'm almost thirteen."

"Where are yer folks?"

"I only have my sister. She's up in New York City."

"No pa and no ma?"

"No."

"No cousins or uncles or other kin?"

"No, they're all in Ireland."

"I know of that, and Scotland, too—over the seas."

Suddenly, Charley felt his knees weakening. He said, "I got to sit down," and sank onto the porch at the woman's bare feet.

This was the signal for the goose to come at him, hissing, beating her wings, making Charley lift his arms to protect his face from her beak.

"Git off him, Malindy. Shoo." Old Jerusha Bent swatted the goose with the broom beside the door, making it flutter down off the porch. She shouted after the bird, "He ain't worth peckin'. No Yankee deserter is." The woman paused to watch the goose flap away, then fold her wings. Now she asked, "Puny as ya are, what'd the Yankees want with ya?"

"They made a drummer boy out of me," Charley said softly. In spite of his fear, he felt shame as he said it.

"And ya say ya run from the fightin' down below?"

"Yes, at the Wilderness."

"I seen it. That's a bad place. It's witched, I'd say." The woman was silent for a long moment, then all at once asked, "Are ya hungry?"

"I said I was. I'll pay you for any food you'll sell me."

"No, ya won't. It ain't yer money I want, Mr. Skedaddle. Come inside and set. If it's eggs ya come after, it's eggs ya'll get."

Charley got up. He waited until Granny Bent put her pistol under her arm, took the lantern, and opened her back door. Then he followed her inside.

In the glow of the hearth fire, he saw a large woman with wild gray hair streaked with black. Her face was brown, wrinkled as a nut meat, and her eyes black, sharp, and fierce-looking. Her shirt was blue calico and her overalls a faded, deeper blue. Suddenly she grinned. Her teeth were white and strong, with spaces between them.

"Red hair and blue eyes. Ya've got spirit, even if ya ain't got grit. That means I got to watch ya good, don' it?"

"Why watch me?" asked Charley.

"Why watch ya? To keep ya handy. I told ya it wasn' yer money I wanted. It's *yerself*! I need a boy here to help me out, and it appears to me ya been sent to Granny Jerusha because she needs ya. Me and Malindy'll keep good watch over ya.

"I wouldn' try to run away if I was ya. The way ya talk, mountain folks would guess ya for a Yankee and it'd go hard for ya. But as long as ya stay here, they won' come meddle with ya. Nobody bedevils a wise woman in the hills."

"What's a wise woman?"

"A part-Indian doctor-woman and a baby-bringer. Some say I cast spells, too." Jerusha Bent chuckled and added softly, "Some'll name ya Witch Boy, but once they know ya belong to me, ya'll be safe enough—never ya fear. If yer Yankees come seeking ya, ya coward of a boy, I'll hide ya from 'em. Ya know, ya'll be best off with me while the war's happenin' below. One peep outa yer mouth will be enough to put an end to ya. I'm savin' yer skin if ya don' have the wits to know it yet. They'd shoot ya down if they could get the matter outa what ya say. Ya ain't so easy to understand, Boy."

Angry at this old woman's ways, Charley flared. "If everybody here hates Yankees so much, why don't you shoot me now?"

Jerusha Bent's dark eyes gleamed. "I been other places than these hills, Boy. I got my reasons not to shoot ya, and they're good ones. Now, there's water over yonder in the jug. That round water carrier ya got on ya marks ya as a Yankee. Git it off now and give it to me. I'll bury it in the mornin'. Once ya've had water, wash yer hands and face before ya eat. And be sure to use the lye soap, Boy. There's a rag on a nail beside the jug to wipe yerself with. If ya wonder what to call me, Granny or ma'am'll do."

Charley had listened carefully to her talk and wondered if she was crazy. Did she even realize what she was saying about spells and witch boys? He'd better be careful.

Trying to humor her, Charley asked, "Are you really an Indian?"

"I didn' say I was. Don' ya listen? I said I'm *part* Indian—one quarter Creek. Remember that. I can tell what yer thinkin', and track ya wherever ya aim to run to. The wise woman does the first part; the Creek does the second. And I ain't one bit crazy like yer thinkin' this very minute, Boy Skedaddle!"

11 WITCH BOY

While he washed himself, Charley looked around him. Old Jerusha Bent certainly didn't live elegantly. Except that it had a shingle roof, her cabin wasn't much better than the one he'd shared with Silas and the others in Culpeper. Like it, hers had a big fireplace with kettles and iron pots at one end and a window at the other. There wasn't much furniture, just a wooden table, two split-bottom chairs, nails to hang clothing on, a spinning wheel, and a bed. The kitchen he'd seen as he came in was just a lean-to off the back porch. At the top of one wall was a loft with a ladder positioned against it. And in the dim light he could just make out a number of brown, green, and yellow bottles with dark-colored twigs and bark in them on the mantel.

With the old woman gone to the lean-to to fix him something to eat, Charley went hopefully to the front door and then to the window, wondering if he could escape through them. The door was barred high up, too high for him to reach, and the window was nailed shut.

No, he couldn't get away—not right now, anyway.

His face and hands dried, Charley sat down at the table to wait. He truly was hungry. He'd eat and then he'd plot his escape. If he'd gotten through the Wilderness unseen, he ought to be able to get through these wooded hills, too.

Granny Bent brought him a plate of eggs, bacon, and corn bread. With it came what was meant to be coffee. She sighed as she gave it to him. "This is parched corn. You Yankees got all the real coffee, don'tcha?" Before Charley could answer, she went on. "I better tell ya there's more'n jest Confed'rate deserters about. There's bandits here, too, men that don' care for no army, north or south. Everythin' that's on the run heads for the mountains. They'd rob ya and shoot ya. Ya seen that there's no gettin' outa my house by the door or winder. The good Lord sent ya here, I'd say to preserve ya."

Listening to this, Charley choked on a bite of corn bread. She had truly read his mind. Bandits, too? These mountains were dangerous—maybe more dangerous than going north of the Wilderness would have been.

She pointed to the loft. "Up there. That's where young'uns old enough to climb the ladder sleep."

Charley nodded, though he knew once he was up there, all she had to do was take the ladder away to hold him prisoner. The old woman said, "There's shucked corn and dried gourds up there. Don' ya lay on 'em. Ya'll find old quilts there."

As Charley finished his food, the woman continued, "I don' let my chickens run wild like most folks do here— when they got chickens at all. That way, I can always lay my hands on a egg, not go huntin' for 'em. I go to bed when they do and get up with 'em."

Charley asked, "If I have to stay here, what'll you want me to do?"

"Plant and hoe and weed and tote water. Help me hunt for yarbs in the woods and help me with the yarbs."

"Yarbs?"

"Sassafras and sarsaparilla and boneset and others. Don'tcha know what yarbs are?"

Charley thought hard on the word *sarsaparilla*. It was a drink he knew. Someone had once told him it was made from an herb. He asked, "Are those herbs?"

"Yarbs. That's what they are. Ain't there any where you come from?"

"No, ma'am, not that I know of."

"Ya'll learn 'em here, then. I do doctorin' with 'em. Give me that round water thing yer totin'."

Charley nodded as he gave up the canteen and drank the bitter parched-corn coffee. Oh, but he was tired from all the uphill walking he'd done that day. The strangeness of the cabin and the old woman wearied him, too. Though he'd be a prisoner, he looked forward to sleeping in the loft.

He asked, "Will I go doctorin' with you?"

"Not when I take out Canaan and go to birthin's. Bringin' babies is women's work."

The boy asked, "Who's Canaan?"

"My mule. That's a Bible name. Can ya read the Bible, Boy?"

"Yes, ma'am."

She sighed. "Ain'tcha the fortunate one? If I had a

113

Bible, ya could read it to me nights because I can't. I'd like ya to read to me from it. It's got the Holy Ghost in it. Are ya a churchly boy?"

Churchly? Did that mean what he thought it meant? Charley said, "I went to Mass sometimes with my sister."

"Mass? I heard of that when I lived below in the bluegrass country. That's churchgoin' for Cath'lics, ain't it?"

"Yes, ma'am."

Her eyes widened. "Lord above, I got me a redheaded Cath'lic Yankee deserter boy here. No matter, it's the same God above that we both got, ain't it?"

"I guess so." Charley ducked his head. She'd called herself a "witch," and yet she was talking about churches. She couldn't truly be a witch and be religious, too, could she?

That night, despite his weariness, Charley lay wide-awake for a long time in the loft. Clear enough, he was a captive of this big, old woman who talked and acted so strangely. On one hand he wanted to escape from her and cross the mountains, but what if she had told him the truth about the bandits and the mountaineers shooting strangers? It could be true. If it was, maybe he'd be better off with her even though he didn't know one thing about farm work. But then, he hadn't known about drumming, either, and he'd learned.

One thing was certain. He'd better keep quiet here in the hills so mountain people wouldn't know he was an "outlander," as she named it, and a Yankee to boot. Well, at least she knew how to feed a hungry boy. Her seven eggs and big piece of corn bread had tasted good and filled him to the top.

Now Charley sat upright. By Jiminy, she hadn't said one word about paying him for his work. Should he ask her tomorrow morning? He frowned. No, he'd better not. That could make her angry again.

The next morning, Charley found out what he was to do. He had to plant corn, and fast, because Granny Bent's rheumatic back and shoulders told her rain was coming soon. Already it was two weeks after the new moon, the right time to be planting corn. She showed Charley the spot of ground that began level, then rose up onto the hill behind her cabin.

"All ya got to do, Boy, is make a hole in the ground between them rocks, drop in seed, and cover it over. For now the sun and the rain'll do the rest. Then later on, ya cull the weeds out of the corn. The field's a mite steep and goes uphill a ways, but not so bad ya'll have to weed standin' up, like in some fields around here. Later on, ya'll plant cabbages. Have ya ever done any plantin' before?"

"No, I never did."

"I reckon ya had to buy ever'thin' ya ate where ya come from."

"Yes, ma'am, we have to. We haven't got any land to grow things on. We live upstairs in a big brown house."

"Do tell!" Her eyes glowed with interest. "Don' ya live downstairs, too, then?"

Charley shook his head. "Somebody else lives there, and somebody else lives up over us."

Jerusha Bent muttered, "Why, ya be stacked like cordwood. How can ya git yer breath so close? Speakin' of cordwood, can ya chop wood?"

"No, I never did that, either. We used to buy our wood and coal."

"Why, ya must buy jest about ever'thin', then."

"I guess so, ma'am." Charley wasn't looking at her but at a patch of flat ground over at the right edge of her property, up against her fence. He pointed to it and said, "It's flatter over there. Wouldn't that be a better place than here for planting things?"

"That's my graveyard."

"Oh." Charley stopped, confused. There weren't any tall, white marble angels here. In fact, there weren't any headstones at all that he could see.

She went on. "God gave me five young'uns and took 'em all back before they was full-growed. That was a long time back since me and Isaac laid 'em all to rest." She sighed deeply.

"Isaac?" asked Charley.

"My man, Isaac Bent." She gestured. "He ain't over there, though. He's laid to rest down near Franklin."

"Where's that?"

"Don'tcha know? Ya musta walked through it gettin' up here."

"I didn't know the names of the places I saw."

"No matter. Isaac dug the well and built the cabin for him and me, and we lived here for a long time. Then we went down to Franklin where he done carpenterin' and I learned how to understand what outlanders were sayin'. That's how come I can understand what ya say so easy." She paused to look up at the pale gray sky. Paler gray mist lay high on the hills. "I never took to Franklin. With so many folks around all the time, it seemed I couldn'

breathe. So I came back up here with Canaan, and I don'
find breathin' hard no more."

Charley looked at her, thinking of the hamlets he'd
gone through the previous day. Why, they couldn't have
had more than two hundred people in any of them. If she
felt crowded here, what would she think of New York
City and the Bowery? He felt he didn't breathe as well
here as he had there. The mountains loomed over him,
threatening him.

He asked, "Don't you ever go to town at all?"

"Once a month or so I take yarbs down to Hearne
Hollow and trade 'em for coal oil."

"Could your husband make a living at carpentry up
here in the hills before you went to Franklin?" From
what he'd seen—no other farms in the distance and no
smoke rising anywhere—Isaac Bent couldn't have had
many buyers for his work.

"Isaac had other work to do. Now don't ask me no
more questions."

Work to do? Besides carpentering? More mystery.
Charley wanted to grin but dared not. For sure, Granny
Bent's husband must have been a whiskey maker. He'd
heard talk in Culpeper camp of how the mountain men
made liquor on the sly because they refused to pay any
government, Confederate or North, the tax they were
supposed to pay on every gallon. They made it in secret
and sold it in secret. Had Isaac Bent made liquor and
then gone to Franklin to sell it?

As if she'd read his mind, the old woman said
suddenly, "My Isaac never made squirrel-head whiskey
in his life. Him and me, we left here because a them

MacRaes. There was six of 'em, and just two Bents, Isaac and his old pa. MacRaes and Bents never did git on well together. Sometimes there was shootin'. Jest before we left, they was takin' potshots at us night and day."

Charley felt the hairs on his neck prickle. These mountaineers were dangerous! Not looking at her, he asked, "Are there still MacRaes and Bents around?"

"Like I told ya, there used to be a whole passel of MacRaes, but the old ones passed on and the young'uns went to war. There's a boy yer age now, Cois, that's all. I'm the last a the Bents. They don't mess with me, though, because they think I'm a witch woman. They could have need a me and they know it. There ain't a doctor for a hunderd miles up or down here. Nobody knows no more how the whole ruction started. If Cois MacRae spies ya, ya might have to fight him. Do ya fight at all, Boy?"

Charley boasted, "I'm a good fighter, ma'am."

"But ya ran away and deserted from yer army?"

Charley's face flamed. "That was different."

She said sharply, "I can see that it was—to ya. Git on with my plantin', Boy. Tie the seed corn to yer belt so ya can reach in for it." And she went back to the cabin.

The rest of that day, Charley worked hard planting corn and ate what Granny Bent brought to him in the field. He soon decided that farm work was not for him. It wasn't only that it was dull, but before long, his arms and back ached as he stooped and bent, working in the poor, rock-strewn soil. This work made him pine for his good life as a Bowery Boy. Why had he run away? He'd been stupid. He saw that now.

118

That night, with the corn planted and a soft rain falling outside the cabin, Charley answered Granny Bent's questions about New York City as best he could. He told her about the traffic on Broadway and amusements about town and in the Bowery. Her eyes grew wide as he spoke of the railroad that came onto Manhattan Island and of the steamer that had brought him here to Virginia. She had never seen a railroad track, nor the sea. She told him she knew of it, though, because mountain singers sang old ballads of England, Scotland, and Ireland where their ancestors had come from more than a century ago. When he spoke of the idea to dig a road beneath the great city of his birth for trains to run on underground, she said she didn't believe a word of it.

Now, for the first time in days, Charley laughed. "It's hard for me to believe, too, ma'am."

Leaning back in her chair, she asked him, "Are there a lot of black folks where ya live?"

Charley thought it an odd question but said, "Not many at all. Are there up here?"

"Not none up here—none at all. No more Indians, either. My ma was the last Creek to die here, and she was only half Indian. Now, it's time for ya to go to bed. Tomorrow I'm takin' ya to Hearne Hollow with me so folks'll git a look at ya and spread the news I got ya for my boy. Don' talk and don' git outa my sight down there. I'll give ya a old jacket I got here to keep ya warm on the way. We'll be startin' early and it'll be cold."

The old woman woke Charley at daybreak by banging the ladder against the edge of the loft. "The rain's over. I got corn bread from last night for ya. Canaan's ready to go. Come on, Skedaddle Boy."

His hair combed with his fingers, his eyes heavy with sleep, his face damp from a hasty wash, Charley set out minutes later with Granny Bent and her black mule. She rode with a basket of yarb bottles in her hand, and Charley followed on foot.

Granny Bent took a trail through laurel thickets that went in another direction from the one that had brought Charley to her farm. This trail twisted about uphill and down, and finally came to a road that skirted the top of a deep ravine. After a time, it swerved to the left and went downhill. After near two hours of travel, they came to a tiny settlement composed of a handful of one-story houses in a pocket in the hills beside a stream.

Hearne Hollow consisted of a stone gristmill to grind corn, a steepled church made of planks, a store, and two other small, unpainted wooden buildings. Two elderly, long-bearded men leaned on the store's fence, and three others sat on its porch, each with a hound dog at his feet. Charley stared at them as he and the old woman came up together. They were lanky men with light eyes and yellowish skins, dressed like Granny Bent was.

"Howdy, Jerusha," one called out as he stopped whittling. "Who's that ya got with ya?"

She called back, "A featherheaded chunk of a boy I found wanderin' in the woods. He don' seem to be able to talk, but he understands good enuf. If he ever gets hisself lost, fetch him back to me. He helps me with my corn. How's yer daughter's new baby, Amos?"

"Keepin' fine, both a 'em, since ya saw 'em last when he got born. What'cha call the boy?"

120

"Boy does good enough for him. Come along inside now, Boy."

While Charley, who disliked being called Boy, looked about and sniffed the strong odors of the store, Granny Bent traded her yarbs for kerosene. He heard her tell the man behind the counter, "This bottle's pinkroot for fevers. That one's spikenard for sore backs, and this one's sassafras and . . ." After that, he stopped listening until he heard her ask, "Is there any news about the war?"

The store owner, a tall man with few teeth and a tobacco-stained beard, spat a stream of tobacco juice out the window behind him and said, "Another conscriptor lookin' for deserters come through here early today. He said there's wild fightin' goin' on now in a place called Spottsylvania Courthouse, not far from the Wilderness. The Wilderness is still burnin' if yestidday's rain didn't put it out."

The Wilderness! Pain and shame caught Charley so sharply, he almost cried out.

Her business finished, Granny Bent went back outside to her mule. There were now two more people on the porch, an old woman and a boy. They all let Granny pass, but when Charley, who was carrying the jug of kerosene, came out, the boy stuck out his bare foot to trip him. Charley saw the foot just in time to escape it by jumping backward.

The yellow-headed, yellow-eyed mountain boy, a whole head taller than Charley, hissed at him, "I'm Cois. I seen ya comin' along the ridge with the old witch woman, so I come down here fast. They say yer her witch boy."

Cois? Cois MacRae. What should he do? Charley asked himself. This was a challenge, one that couldn't be overlooked. He set the jug down carefully and then looked to Granny Bent, who was beside Canaan and watching him.

Charley caught the nod of her head. It was a signal to fight. Fight! She'd said he might have to because she was a Bent. It wasn't fair, though. He wasn't a Bent. Well, he supposed this wouldn't be much different from a Bowery Boy fighting a Dead Rabbit back home. Lots of other things up here seemed strange and different, but this he understood. Charley nodded, then he put up his fists just as he would have done in Chatham Square.

12 VISITORS!

Cois MacRae didn't fight the way Charley expected him to, like a real bare-knuckle champion would. He didn't come forward with his fists raised. Instead, he darted for Charley's legs and brought him down onto his face. Instantly, the mountain boy rolled away from Charley and then grabbed him by a flailing leg and turned him over onto his back. In another instant, Cois was straddling Charley, pinioning his arms and bouncing up and down on his stomach, knocking the air out of him. "I kotched ya. I kotched ya, witch boy," he chanted as Charley thrashed his legs about and tried to free his arms. "Kotched ya good, I did, ya outlander witch boy. I can spit in yer face whenever I wants to."

It was Granny Bent who stopped Charley's humiliation. She came up to Cois, grabbed him by his long hair, and gave him a swat across the side of his head. She cried at him, "My boy don' know mountain rasslin'. Git up off him, Cois."

"Git away from me, ya pizen female."

"Ya git off my boy or I'll lay a spell on ya so ya'll never grow taller than ya are right now and ya won't never get what ya want. Swallow yer spit."

While the old mountaineers chuckled, Cois got up reluctantly. Charley rose up quickly and looked shame-faced at Granny Bent, whose dark eyes raked his face. She told him, "Come along now, Boy. Don' forgit my coal-oil jug."

As he followed her, Charley heard the snickers of the old men and the call to his rescuer. "Yer boy don' appear to be a much use, Jerusha. Can't talk and can't fight. Take him home and feed him up to be worth somethin'."

To Charley's relief, Jerusha Bent didn't pay any heed to what had been said. She swung up onto Canaan and started away. Charley followed with the kerosene at the black mule's tail. It wasn't until they were out of sight of the settlement that the old woman halted. For a long moment she looked at Charley, then she said, "Ya were aimin' to fight him, wasn' ya?"

"Yes, but I didn't know he'd fight that way."

"Ya do now, Boy."

Charley spoke bitterly. "Next time I'll move in first and hit him on the nose."

"I think ya will. What'll be yer reasons?"

"Because I don't like the way he fights and because of what he called me—and you."

"Reasons enough right there." She smiled crookedly, turned around, and called back over her shoulder, "If that kerosene gits too heavy for ya, put it in one of Canaan's saddlebags."

"It won't get too heavy for me."

As they went uphill, Charley thought about what he'd heard of the war. He knew where Spottsylvania was from a map he'd seen at the Culpeper camp headquarters. It lay eastward and not too far from the Wilderness. So the two great armies were still in the state. He wondered who had won the last battle, and who would win at this new one, Generals Grant and Meade or the white-haired, bearded General Lee he'd seen atop the gray horse. That old man had been going right into the scrap. He'd had courage and plenty of it. Tears of shame came to Charley's eyes, making it hard for him not to stumble in the ruts of the narrow road. He knew he'd cry again, too, but he vowed he would never weep in front of Granny Bent.

July came in with a blaze of scarlet, purple, and gold wild flowers so vivid that they took Charley's breath away. For sheer beauty, the mountains beat New York City. The various greens of the many trees, the brilliance of the stars as they sprang out of the darkening sky, and the bluish mists that clung to the slopes enchanted Charley in spite of his homesickness and the constant ache in his soul for deserting. Soon he began to recognize the calls of the mountain birds. The deer that came fearlessly to feed in the Bent meadow at dusk filled him with awe. Granny Bent never shot an animal. One time, as he hunted "yarbs" with her, he spied a black bear sitting on a bald spot in a great hill warming himself, his huge shaggy head lifted to the morning sun. The sight had delighted him. On the other hand, the venomous snakes Granny Bent pointed out filled him with horror.

She caught him once, using the rosary the priest had given him at Culpeper, and she had listened as he explained it. Then she had said, "I say there's a power in prayer. Be careful what you pray for, Boy. I aim to take ya to church with me the end of this month. A travelin' preacher's comin', and there's to be a footwashin'."

Ever mindful of the danger to him here in the hills, Charley obeyed Granny's order not to speak when callers "helloed" the cabin and came for medicines or brought her game they had killed. He would go to the shed and sit with Canaan until they had gone, then come out and go about his work.

The third week in July, by his reckoning of time since the Battle of the Wilderness, the old woman was summoned to a "birthing." A girl Charley's age came riding bareback on an old swayback mare to the house. Charley had been at the point of leaving for the shed when he heard her call out, "Granny, my sister's time's come. Can ya come with me now?"

"I'll fetch what I need, Sarie Giffen, saddle up my mule, and be with ya soon as I lock up Boy in the henhouse."

Sarie Giffen had shining black curls and pale blue eyes. Her ragged dress had once been rose-colored calico but was now gray. Her feet were dirty, but her ankles were milk-white. She was the prettiest girl Charley had ever seen, and he gawked at her.

"Do ya got to lock him up, Granny?" asked the girl, staring at Charley.

"I better. He might run off and get lost. Come along, Boy."

As Charley went with her, he knew she meant to say "run away," and he would, too. Twice that day Granny Bent had reminded him he was a coward and a deserter. Sometimes Charley thought he was almost starting to like her, and then she gave him the rough edge of her tongue, so he felt the same way toward her again.

The henhouse was just big enough for the hens to roost and for him to lie down on the quilt she'd given him before she locked the door with a big, old metal lock. He couldn't squirm out of the hole the hens came in and out of because it was too small. He had to sit there with corn bread and water until she came back.

Granny Jerusha had left with the pretty girl at noon and didn't come back until daybreak the next morning. First of all, she let Charley out, then told him to look to Canaan in the shed.

Charley asked, "Was the baby a boy or a girl?"

"Another boy. I heard it said in wartime lotsa boys get birthed." Her eyes were cold. "He'll be some fool of a willie to run off to war someday soon as he hears they're gatherin' soldiers. Men like war. It makes 'em feel big. There's nothin' so bad it can't be talked out without fightin'. But some do dote on fightin'."

Charley shook his head. He hadn't liked war at all— not once he'd gotten a taste of it.

Granny Bent repeated, eyeing him, "Oh, lots of 'em like it jest fine. I reckon ya did, too, for a time. Think on it."

As he took Canaan to the shed, Charley did think. He'd been eager to fight to avenge Johnny—at first. Other men never seemed to lose that eagerness. Look at

Silas and the three generals he had seen. You bet they liked it! You could tell by the way they acted and talked. Granny Bent was right, but would he ever tell her so? Never.

Another birthing call came toward the end of the month at dawn. Once more Charley was locked in the henhouse. He resented this now more than ever. The old woman ought to start trusting him. He'd dug a hole for a new privy for her, planted her cabbage seeds, weeded and watered her fast-growing corn, curried her mule, fed her hens, hunted herbs in the forest with her and then ground them into a powder, helped her make lye soap, boiled quilts outside in a big iron pot over a fire, washed yarb bottles—he'd done everything she required of him and never once talked back. Charley hated being locked up, and this time he'd do something about it.

Through a chink in the henhouse wall, he watched Granny Bent and an old mountaineer ride off together. Then, smiling, he went to the opening the hens and rooster used. He knew the old wood there was rotten. He pried the wood apart and squeezed through the much larger space. Grinning, he propped up the rotten boards where they had been before, making them seem natural.

Now he took the path that led to Hearne Hollow. Down there he'd spotted a road that led in the direction he figured was west. He'd circle around the settlement, go along that road—and goodbye and fare-thee-well to Jerusha Bent!

He was halfway there when he heard a hoarse shout, "Stand where y'are, boy," and saw a rifle barrel pushed out from behind a tree trunk.

Charley froze and waited.

The voice came again. "Y'are Granny Bent's boy, the one that can't talk, ain'tcha?"

What should he do? Run for it? No, better not. He nodded.

"Are ya lost, boy?"

Charley nodded again.

"Never ya mind. I'll take ya back to her place." And out from behind the tree stepped a lanky old man with a stiff gray beard under a wide black hat. Charley recognized him at once as one of the men he'd seen on the porch last month down in the settlement. "Git back up the trail. I'll tell ya which way to go."

So Charley, his hopes blasted, was driven back to the Bent farm. There the old mountaineer left him with the words, "Don' wander off no more or somebody'll take the notion to shoot ya. The hills is full of squirrel hunters now."

Again Charley nodded and sat down. He waited on the porch listening to the cicadas and crickets until at dusk he saw Canaan and Granny returning. Then he ran to the henhouse, squeezed back inside, and put the rotten boards up again. When the old woman let him out, she was none the wiser about his adventure.

The final Sunday in July, Granny Bent took him to Hearne Hollow to church. Washed, wearing a clean shirt, Charley sat on a backless bench next to her, marveling at how different this mountain church was from the one he'd gone to in New York City. Where were the statues of Christ, the Virgin Mary, and the saints? Where were the stained-glass windows or the paintings of the Stations of the Cross? Where was the sweet incense and the altar boys and the choir and the fine vestments for the priest? How plain this was. Here everything was white, brown, and black—whitewashed walls, brown benches, and dingy black and gray clothing with the strong smell of lye soap about them. There was no beautiful singing. First came the twanging of the tuning fork, then the voices of the mountaineers, singing not in Latin but in English. Some of the women had good voices, but they scarcely could be heard over the growling bass of the visiting preacher, a big, white-headed man in a black coat and tattered trousers.

After the service came the most astonishing thing of all, the foot-washing. Some older people took off their shoes and had their feet washed in basins of water and dried with towel rags by others. No one washed Charley's feet or ordered him to wash anyone's, but Granny Bent's feet got washed by Sarie Giffen, and Cois MacRae washed the horny yellow ones of an old, old man.

When that was over, there was a sort of party on the porch of the store. Most of the families that had come down from hillside farms had brought food with them: cooked pork and corn bread, buttermilk, wild honey from bee trees, and lard-crust berry pies. Nobody invited Charley to sit down until Sarie Giffen came up to him, took his hand, and led him to where she and her family—her older sister, her sister's war-wounded husband, and their three little ones—were sitting with Granny Bent. Sarie sat him down beside a small, black-haired boy, filled his hands with food, then sat a distance away on a step crooning to her sister's just-baptized new baby. As Charley ate, Sarie smiled at him now and then. What a peach she was, thought Charley. If only he could talk to her, but he didn't dare open his mouth except to shove food into it.

After a while, he saw Cois MacRae go over to Sarie and say something into her ear. Whatever he had said made Sarie angry. She scowled and then swung about and hit Cois hard on the ear with her open hand. Everybody who saw her do it laughed, while Cois glowered with rage.

Now Charley got up slowly. He walked over to Cois and the girl and stood waiting, his hands in his pockets. He locked eyes with Cois, who glared back at him. Charley recalled what Johnny had once told him—watch for the light in a man's eyes that tells you when he's going to make his move in a fight.

There was the flicker he'd waited for. Like a flash, Charley's right hand came out of his pocket to hit Cois full on the nose. Then, as Cois doubled over, he hit him in the stomach and Cois went down. Not for long, though. He was soon up, ready to rush Charley and "rassle" him.

This time the visiting preacher stopped the fight, thrusting himself between the boys. His powerful hands shot out east and west as he grabbed each by the neck, brought their heads together, and cracked them hard. As he did, he bellowed, "There won't be no ruction on the Lord's Day!"

"*Boy!*" called Granny Bent the minute the minister let Charley go, flinging him away. His head ringing with pain, a dizzy Charley wove his way over to her and sat down where she patted. She asked him so softly that nobody else heard her amid all the laughter, "Do ya think ya had a good reason to hit Cois?"

Charley nodded firmly, his eyes blazing with joy for what he had just done. He'd gotten even with the mountain boy, and everybody here who had been there the first time knew it.

Charley turned toward Sarie. The girl was rocking back and forth on the step with the baby, not looking at anyone. The white skin of her face had turned to a rose red, though. Was she angry with him? He hoped not. He'd meant well by her. As he looked, she turned her head and gave him a quick little grin.

He next turned his gaze toward Cois, who sat between two old men. The boy was holding a rag to his bloody nose. He was looking at the rag, not at Charley.

All at once Charley realized that this fight wasn't like the ones he'd had with Dead Rabbits in the Bowery. He'd fought there because it was the expected way to act toward a rival gang. Here he'd fought because he guessed Cois had said something bad to Sarie. Yes, this *was* different! This was a fight he had chosen to fight because somebody else had been hurt.

Charley Quinn felt good about himself!

13 A SPECIAL VISITOR

By August, Charley was able not only to recognize some of the trees, but also to identify a number of the herbs that grew in the mountains, learning which leaves and berries to avoid. To his astonishment, some like the pokeweed could be poisonous in some part of the plant at certain times of the year and not at others. Others looked harmless but were in fact deadly. Yet others made poultices powerful enough to cause a blister. One in particular, called dew pizen, was extremely dangerous. One scratch from it made an arm or leg swell up and turn black.

As they roamed the mountains together, Charley became more and more at ease with old Jerusha, though she still locked him in her henhouse when she went to birthings. In turn, he played his game of getting out, waiting till he saw her at a distance, then going back in among the hens. There was no telling how she might act if she caught him sitting on the porch patting Malindy, who turned out to be as tame as any dog.

August nights were beautiful in the hills. Sometimes Charley felt he was in a dream. He learned to like to sit on the steps of the creaking porch and look up at the silvery fire of the stars and hear the old woman tell him their names. Granny Bent knew not only the names of many of the constellations and just about every plant and tree, but also the songs and night calls of mountain birds. To entertain her, Charley tried to imitate some of them. To his joy, now and then a bird would answer. He vowed to remember the birds' songs, and someday, God willing, he'd imitate them at home for Noreen.

His sister seemed very far away from him here in the Virginia hills. He could perhaps send a letter from the tiny post office in Hearne Hollow to somewhere else in the South, but never one to New York City in the North. Not only would it never get sent, but worse than that, it would mark him at once as a hated Yankee. He only hoped that Noreen would sense he was still alive. His face burned as with fever whenever he thought of what Captain Mahoney or someone else might have written about his behavior in the battle.

What was happening in the war? Nobody who came to Granny Bent's farm seemed to have any news of what was happening in the eastern part of the state. Who had won at Spottsylvania? Where was new fighting going on? One thing only Charley did know for certain—the Confederate conscriptor patrols were still out and about hunting up deserters. Every couple of weeks echoing horns answered one another throughout the mountains as families warned their deserter relatives to take cover.

That would not be difficult for them, he knew. These

hills had not only enormous tangled thickets of mountain laurel and rhododendron, but also caves in the very rocks themselves. A whole army could hide in these mountains. One man could take his pick of shelters and move every night. Although he and Granny Bent never encountered a Johnny Reb deserter while they were out "yarb" gathering, Charley sensed watchful eyes on the two of them.

Jerusha Bent felt them, too. Once, when they were on their hands and knees digging up snakeroot, she whispered to Charley, "Don' turn around, Boy. There's somebody over there."

"A man?" Charley whispered back.

"Yes, he's watchin' us."

"Is he a bandit?" Charley took tight hold of his knife.

"No, they don' go around alone. Mebbe he's a deserter, or mebbe he's got hisself a still around here. Let's leave this root and go. He's got a squirrel rifle with him. Jest get up and walk away now."

Fearfully, Charley obeyed. Granny Bent had told him all about stills, an apparatus that made whiskey from grain and fruit. Men who had stills, she said, were mighty touchy about folks coming too near. More than one careless mountain boy had gotten himself shot by angry whiskey-makers who took no chances. And the same mountaineer who shared his kill of elk, bear meat, or venison with his neighbors might drive them off with bullets the very next day for coming too near his still. By now, Charley had given up the notion that Granny's husband had been a moonshine-maker. But what else had he done?

*   *   *

One late August night just before dusk, Charley sat on the porch as usual while Granny Bent rocked in a noisy old rocking chair. As night came down, they listened to the noises of insects and birds, watching the peaks surrounding them turn purple-dark and the full moon rise over them. Then suddenly, Charley heard a birdcall he'd not heard before. Granny Jerusha heard it, too. The sounds of her rocking stopped and she half rose from it to peer into the growing darkness.

"What's that one?" asked Charley. "I never heard it before."

"I have—a long time ago. It don' belong up here. It's a bluegrass-country bird."

"What's it called?"

"I don' know the name of it. Mebbe it's some kind of owl. Best go see to the hens. Owls like chickens. Stay with 'em, Boy."

An owl? No owl sounded like this.

"Go to the hens, Boy!" the old woman repeated firmly.

Charley got up and walked around the side of the house past the chopping block. He lifted up the latch of the henhouse and went inside to check on the chickens, asleep on their roosting perches. Moonlight flooding in from the open door made a rectangle on the floor. By its light, he counted the fowls. Not one was missing.

All at once, the door was closed behind him and the lock attached. Granny Bent had followed him and locked him in. Why? She hadn't been called away to bring a baby tonight.

He felt his anger rise. He waited till she'd gone, then he pushed aside the old boards and got out. Carefully, he circled the house and stopped alongside it, pressing his back to the logs. He could hear voices from inside. Keeping his head down, Charley crept to the window and then very cautiously lifted his head to peek inside.

There was a man in there with the old woman, a broad-backed man in a dark coat. Who was he? Where had he come from? There wasn't any horse or mule tethered anywhere that he could see. Whoever this was, he'd come on foot. Why? What did he want? Now Charley thought he knew about that birdcall. It hadn't been a bird at all. Granny Bent had known what it was and gotten rid of him. Why?

The cabin light was dim, but by its feeble glow, he saw Jerusha embracing the man. Her arms went around him and his arms around her. He saw the man lift her off the floor and heard her laugh. Then she kissed him on the cheek.

Finally, they parted and Charley was able to see her caller from the side. He gasped. It was a man in a dark coat with a line of buttons down its front. A Union Army coat! On his head he wore a visored cap.

He was a black man, a Yankee soldier, way up here in the mountains! There hadn't been any black troops at the Wilderness with him, though he'd heard there were some elsewhere in northern Virginia. He'd read in the newspapers in New York that Abe Lincoln was recruiting blacks for his army and had seen some in New York City, but this man was the first black soldier he'd ever seen this far south. Why was he here?

The pair of them talked at some length. Then the old woman went to the hearth, took up some ash cakes left over from supper, and gave them to the black visitor.

137

They talked again for five or ten minutes, then the man went to the door, peered out, and swiftly ran down off the porch and disappeared into the forest.

For sure, that black man must be a Yankee deserter, too! But look how he'd been greeted—like a son. Granny Bent hadn't met him with a pistol and harsh words as she'd met Charley. No, he wouldn't go back to the henhouse, squeeze inside, and wait to be let out, not after what he'd just seen! Charley walked stiff-legged to the door, opened it, and went in.

As the old woman looked up in astonishment at seeing him, he told her accusingly, "Who was that? I saw you in here with that black soldier. How come you treated him so well and me so bad? He's a deserter, too, isn't he?"

By now, Granny Bent had recovered herself. She sat down at her table and motioned Charley over to her. "That was Thad Porter ya saw just now. He's grown big. Last time I saw him, he was yer size. He ain't no deserter, he's a soldier. Isaac and me, we knew him twenty years back and helped him and his sister. He got leave to pay me a call jest now. Sit down, Boy."

Not a deserter? Charley sat down, marveling. Had the war come here to the mountains? He hadn't heard any cannon fire, a sound that carried for miles. "Where's he going?" asked Charley.

"Back to his unit. It's in the east part of the state. There was a battle at a place called Cold Harbor. He says they got the Confederates bottled up real good not far from Richmond."

Charley stared at her in surprise. She was smiling. *She looked glad!* Why should news that was bad for the South please her?

He said, "You're *glad* about that?"

She nodded. "I don' hold with keepin' folks in bond-age."

"But aren't you afraid Thad will get shot by somebody up here who hates the Yankees?"

"Don't ya worry about him. Thad'll git away with nobody seein' him. He knows all the paths hereabouts. Isaac showed 'em to him when Thad and his sister were up here as young'uns. He risked his life to come see me now."

That was true, Charley admitted. He asked, "Why did he come?"

"To tell me how he's doin' and to let me know that his sister's goin' to school up North to be a nurse. We had 'em for a time. They got like family to me and Isaac." Suddenly Jerusha Bent grinned at Charley and asked, "Ain'tcha never heard of the Underground Railroad, Boy?"

The Underground Railroad? Of course he knew about it. Who didn't in the northern states? Noreen and Johnny had talked about the secret organization that helped black men and women escape from slavery. They were passed along from "station" to "station" on the invisible road to the North and freedom.

"Were *you* in the Underground Railroad?" Was this the mystery Granny Bent had kept from him about what else her Isaac had done?

She nodded. "Yes. Isaac and me, we was a station on it for fifteen years—until jest before we went down to Franklin to git away from the MacRaes. Black folks were fetched to us by somebody up here, and we brought 'em on to a place farther north of us. Isaac and me, we risked goin' to prison by helpin' slaves that had run away, but we done it all the same. Now Thad's risked his life to ride clear across the state to see me. I don' know how he talked the Army into lettin' him come, but he did. Now tell me how ya got outa the henhouse." She was smiling at him.

"I'll show you in the morning." Charley relaxed at her smile. "You don't need to lock me in there anymore. I've been getting out for weeks when you go away. I won't go anywhere without you, don't worry. Everybody knows I'm your boy—just Boy, that's all." Charley mumbled this last part, looking at his work-scarred hands. After a moment, he added, "It took a real brave man to do what Thad did."

"You bet, and he did it all alone without anyone cheerin' him on. That's truly bein' brave. Thad's got sand in his gizzard."

And I don't have any sand—that's what she was just about to say, thought Charley Quinn. How she must despise him for being a deserting, skedaddling coward. He got up and went out the back door of the cabin, leaving the old woman at the table. He couldn't bear to have her call him "coward" to his face again. The fights he'd fought with Cois MacRae didn't mean anything compared to what Thad Porter had done. What did he have to be proud of? Charley sat down on the back porch to look at the dark mountainside rising above the corn-field and the Bent graveyard. He thought about Jem Miller and Silas Gorman and his hero brother and now Thad Porter. How insignificant he was in comparison to them.

14

CHRISTMAS AND THE CRITTER

The next morning, Charley showed Granny Bent the rotten boards of the chicken coop that permitted him to get out and in. She didn't have the scalding words for him he halfway expected to get. She only looked critically at the old wood and said, "Ya'd best put in new ones today, or some animal that fancies hen meat or eggs'll git in by pushin' hard. There's plenty of 'em about."

"Yes, ma'am, I will," Charley said. He added, "Are you still going to lock me up when you go out bringing babies?"

Old Jerusha shook her head and laughed. "There don' seem to be much cause to do that when ya could have run off anytime ya wanted to after ya got fetched back here that one time."

Charley gaped at her. She knew about that?

She was smiling at him. "I know. Ever'thin' that goes on here in the hills gits talked about. That's because there ain't ever much news. Ever'body talked about how Jerusha's wool-headed outlander boy got hisself lost and had to be fetched home else he'd never find his way back. They say yer quiet and hide yer lack a brains by keepin' still. Now, Boy, fix them boards before ya take water buckets to the corn."

Angered at the insults, Charley went to work with an ax to cut and shape boards to repair the hole, then he took hammer and nails to the boards he'd made. As he worked, he thought how different this was from delivering the hats Noreen had trimmed in New York City. His anger gradually faded away. Look what he could do with his hands in the few months he'd been up here when before he hadn't been able to do a single thing that needed doing on the farm. He was proud of what he could do. No Bowery Boy could chop wood or hoe corn like he could, or fix leaks in a shingle roof. Any of them could deliver hats to fancy stores on Broadway.

After he fixed the hole, Charley stood back to admire it. He'd done a good job. He'd call Granny Bent to look at it. After all, it hadn't been her calling him "wool-headed." It had probably been that old mountaineer who had caught him on the trail.

In the weeks that followed, there was no mention by the mountain folk who came to the Bent farm that there had been any black Union Army soldier caught and killed. So Thad must have gotten away safely. For once Charley was happy that he didn't hear any war news.

And, except for that extraordinary visit, one day was very much like the one preceding it. Charley found that the days grew timeless to him. Johnny's watch meant little here, though the boy kept it wound up and working.

Time was marked off by getting up, doing chores, and going to bed, or by visitors coming to see Granny Bent.

While he watered the growing corn and the little crop of cabbages, and later shucked the corn to store in the crib and put the harvested cabbages in the loft, a steady trickle of mountaineers arrived on foot or muleback to consult with Granny Jerusha. They'd tell her, "I don' feel so pert, Granny," or, "I feel weak and nervish," or, "I'm worn out clear through," or, "My legs keep poorly," and she'd give them a bottle of this yarb or a pinch of that. Sometimes they paid her with paper money printed by the Confederate government in Richmond, but mostly they gave her a jar of wild honey, a side of bacon, or a basket of blackberries, wild strawberries, or huckleberries.

Charley worked each day on the farm, and soon autumn arrived. It came in colors so bright, they made his eyes ache to look at them—the orange of sassafras, the flaming scarlet of maples, the deep red of oaks, and the golden yellow of birch. The air was sharp and crisp—to Charley's way of thinking, very like the apples he picked, sliced, and laid on the roof of the cabin to dry for winter use.

Jerusha Bent took him with her to Hearne Hollow twice that fall. The first time they went to have her corn ground into meal at the gristmill and to exchange yarbs for needles and thread, a length of red flannel cloth, some turpentine, and more kerosene for the lantern. Charley didn't see Cois MacRae there or Sarie, either—just two old men whittling on the store steps and letting the chips fall on their sleeping dogs. Nobody had any news of the war.

The second time Charley, the old woman, and Canaan made the trip to the Hollow was weeks later to attend church again. Granny Bent had heard that a new circuit-riding preacher was due, and she and Charley went to hear him. A little, balding man, this minister was a "hell-roarer." He shouted that "devilmint was everywhere," "laziness was bred in the bone," and nobody ever "drowned hisself in sweat." With just about every other statement he made, people called out "Amen" and nodded their heads. Charley marveled at this sort of churchliness, so different from his own attendance at Mass, where each service was like another and he knew what to expect.

Yet he had to agree with the circuit rider that there was devilmint about and laziness aplenty in the world. He'd seen these things in the Bowery and hadn't had to come to the hills to learn it. All the same, the shouting and loud singing here embarrassed him a little, though he sensed the mountaineers were serious in their faith and surely seemed to have a good time in church.

After the service and some baptizing in the nearby creek, the parish gathered around the minister. Because he rode about the hills, a circuit rider often had news to tell. Charley walked up with Granny Bent just as someone asked, "What's happenin' with the war?"

The minister folded his arms and said, "It's still a-fightin'. The Yankees, cuss-ed be their name, have got our Virginny boys holed up at Petersburg in front of Richmond. In Georgia, the town a Atlanta's been taken by the bluebellies, and our men there have gone away to Tennessee, I hear tell. There'll be a-fightin' there before winter, too, I reckon."

Charley backed away. The fighting was *still* going on. It pained him to hear of the war, but it would have pained him more not to know what was happening.

By November, the glorious colors of the trees were gone. Leafless brown branches stood amid the dark stands of pine, cedar, and hemlock. Charley heard wild geese and ducks flying high over the mountaintops as he lay in the loft. The ladder was in its regular place even at night now, so he could climb down and go to the privy or check on the hens if he heard noises in the night. Winter was coming, and with it there would be snow. It would cover the mountains, perhaps until the end of February, and would make the roads all but impassable. Few mountain people would climb to the farm unless led to it by desperate trouble.

Charley had seen snow before in New York City, but there its clear whiteness was soon turned to a brown slush by the feet of people and horses and wagon wheels. Here, when snow came, he found it made the mountains shining white, with the only notes of color the dark evergreens. When the sun shone on it, the snow sparkled in jewellike tones that he'd seen only once before when he'd gone on an errand for a Bowery saloon owner to Tiffany's jewelry store.

Here in the mountains, the sixth of January, Epiphany, was Christmas Day, not December twenty-fifth. He didn't know why, and Granny Jerusha couldn't tell him when he asked.

To Charley's way of thinking, this was a very strange Christmas. Granny Bent didn't seem to prepare for it at all. Because he was with her so much, he couldn't help but see that she wasn't knitting anything that could be a gift. His stockings were worn out now, and he could sure use a new pair, but she didn't knit even one for him so he could hang it up on her chimney as he had always done in New York.

Well, all the same, she would get a gift from him! Because he could whittle some, something he'd done to kill the time on street corners in the Bowery, he whittled her a red-grained wood whistle from a nice piece of wood he cut from a tree.

The morning of January sixth, he gave it to her with the words, "This is a whistle. If you need me while I'm gathering yarbs out in the woods with you, blow on it so I'll hear you."

"And ya'll come to me, Skedaddle?"

"Yes'm, I'll come."

"Thank ya kindly for it." She looked steadily at him and then put the whistle into her shirt pocket.

After that Charley volunteered, "On Christmas Day at home we go to Mass and then give each other presents. After that we go visiting people we know, and we always have a real fine Christmas dinner when we can afford to have one, roast goose or roast beef."

"Do tell! All those goings-on in one day! Malindy wouldn' like hearin' that about the goose. We don' fuss so much here in the hills, but we do eat a good supper, and we sing some, and outside a feedin' the livestock we don' do no work. I ain't got no gift for ya, but I'll feed ya fine today."

Charley had to admit that the highlight of the day was the dinner, the best he'd ever eaten here—a tender ham they'd salted down the previous summer and now soaked in water, then baked; and a lard crust pie from sun-dried apples.

After they finished eating, Granny Jerusha sang a mountain carol to Charley in her harsh, deep, old woman's voice.

In turn, Charley sang a carol in Latin which the sisters had taught him. At its end, Granny Bent said, "Ya got a sweet voice." Then she went on to sing him another carol, "The Cherry Tree Carol," about the tree that at the request of the Baby Jesus let liquid flow off its bent branches to water the thirsty, kneeling animals at the manger.

When she finished, she got up from her chair, took the long rifle down from its pegs above the mantel, and gave it to Charley. She said, "They's one more thing we jest got to do now. I'll take the pistol and shoot her off, and you'll fire this old gun of Isaac's pa."

"Why?" asked Charley.

"It's something we allus do on Christmas Day. I forgot to do it New Year's Eve like I should have. I dunno why hill folks do. Mebbe it's to scare off bad spirits that could be around, mebbe not."

Charley stared at the huge rifle. It was almost as tall as he was. Could he even get it to his shoulder? Would it explode when he fired it? Or kick him back harder than Canaan could?

He feared the huge antique but did not want to let on to Granny Bent. He surely didn't want to be called "coward boy" again. Thank heaven he didn't need to aim it—just fire it.

Outside in the glistening sunset, Granny Bent fired her old pistol into the air, sending a flock of crows flapping out of her apple trees. Knowing it was his turn, Charley put the rifle to his shoulder with difficulty, said a prayer to the Virgin Mary, found the trigger, closed his eyes, and pulled. *Bang!* When he opened his eyes to the smell of gunpowder and the sound of Jerusha Bent's laughter, he realized that he'd been knocked over onto his back from the recoil.

"Ya done it, Charley! I knew ya could! When we get back inside, I'll show ya how to clean and load it again in case ya ever need to use it."

"Do you think I'll need to?" Charley asked ruefully as he got up, brushed snow off his shirt and trousers, and then picked up the long rifle.

"Ya might. There could be bandits come here because there's nobody to rob on the roads now, or there could be critters."

"Critters?"

"Animals, wild ones—hungry, too!"

"Bears?"

The old woman shook her head. "No, bears sleep out the winter and come out in the springtime. Painters—that's what I mean. There's one that's come here the last two winters. Folks call it Old Wry-foot 'cause she's got a twisted paw. It's a her—somebody spied her with cubs one time."

Charley thought of the mountain animals he'd seen over the months—deer, elk, wildcats, bear, raccoons, possums, rabbits, and foxes. Had he seen a "painter," too? "What does a painter look like?"

148

"Like a big yeller cat, lots bigger'n a wildcat—longer'n ya are, Charley. Ya don' gen'rally see 'em, but ya can hear 'em. They let out a yell like a person scared to death."

Like a human screaming? Charley thought back to two nights before. Yes, he'd heard a cry like that while he lay in his loft, half asleep. He had thought it was some winter bird he didn't know. The cry had sounded like a small child, scared and lost. He'd listened for it to come again, but it had not. A big yellow cat? Now he recalled seeing a big yellow animal pacing in a cage at Barnum's show last year. The sign over it had said MOUNTAIN LION—PUMA OR PANTHER. Panther? Was *painter* mountain talk for *panther*? He supposed it was.

Wading through drifts behind her, careful not to let the long rifle drag in the snow, Charley came back to the cabin and set the old weapon on the table to watch its reloading. It surely was a powerful piece, he figured. He looked at it in distaste, though, recalling how he'd delighted in the many shooting galleries of the Bowery. After the Battle of the Wilderness, he didn't want any more shooting. The face of the Confederate he'd shot with Jem Miller's musket rose up over and over again to haunt him. It was like a scene from a play at Niblo's Theater except that it was played over and over in his head, not only during the day but at night in the evil dreams that tormented him.

"Watch me now, Charley," ordered Jerusha Bent as she got the hanging powder horn, a box of cloth patches from the mantel, and the ramrod beside the fireplace. "I got to put in the gunpowder, ya see. . . ."

Suddenly, Charley noticed something. She was using his name now—not Boy. Granny Bent had given him a Christmas present, after all!

He slept well that night, dreamlessly for a change, until the early hours. Then suddenly, he was awakened by the sounds of honking, followed by an unearthly cry. The sounds came from somewhere nearby. He sat bolt upright in his quilts, his heart thudding.

From below he heard Jerusha's voice. "That's the painter I told ya about. She's come back, and Malindy knows she's here. Don' fret over Malindy. That goose is smart enough to fly outa her way."

"What does the painter want?"

"Anythin' livin' she can eat. Don' fret over them hens, neither. Ya fixed up the henhouse good. There ain't no call to git up. The critter can't git in, and she'll be gone before sunrise. Ya'll see her tracks in the mornin', and they'll be big ones, too. I seen 'em last year. Because she's wry-footed, she prob'ly don' hunt so good, so she comes around people's cabins to see what she can get easy-like."

Though Charley lay down again, he could not sleep. When the next wail sounded, he sensed the panther was at the very edge of the cornfield—and that wasn't far from the house.

15 THE LONG NIGHTS

The next morning, sure enough, there were marks of three large paws in the hardened snow, along with one twisted to the left. "Bigger'n last year. It's that same critter I told ya about." Jerusha Bent shook her head as she spoke.

"Granny, what does a painter do in the daytime?"

"Holes up and sleeps somewheres. Nighttimes, she comes out to hunt."

"Will she come back here again?"

"Mebbe so. Mebbe tonight—mebbe a couple days from now. This 'un could visit a couple a farms. Painters got cunning."

"Would she attack a person?"

"Why not? All a person is to a painter is meat."

"Then why didn't you shoot her when she came last year?"

The old woman fixed Charley with her fierce eyes. "Because she ain't hurt me or nothin' a mine so far. Some folks around here shoot and kill for the sake a killin'. I don' hold with that. Have ya seen me shoot anythin'?"

"No, but you eat meat people bring us."

"That's payment for the doctorin' I do for 'em. There ain't much money in these hills—less now than there was afore the war. We got to trade. Hunters pay me in what they got—meat—and I can't tell 'em no."

Charley changed the subject. "Why isn't there any money up here?"

"There's some paper money, but comin' from the Confed'rate government, it ain't worth much. Silver and gold and copper's what I'm talkin' about."

"I've got some money—Yankee money, silver and pennies. If you need any, I'll give you some."

"Keep yer money, Charley. I ain't got no use for it so long as I keep on tradin' for my needs. It's kindly of ya to offer it to me when I never offered to pay ya for the work ya do and kept ya locked up. I do begin to believe yer a better boy than I thought at first."

"Is that because I'm a Yankee and you used to be in the Underground Railroad?"

"No, it ain't. It comes from gettin' to know ya better. Now let's go see how Canaan did with that critter a-howlin' around last night."

January of the new year, 1865, passed without the panther returning to the Bent cabin, though Charley heard her crying on the mountain behind the farm a couple of times. February entered with winds, and as the temperature slowly began to climb, the snow started to disappear. The gentle rains that fell mid-month melted even more of the snow. The Bent farm took on a patchwork-quilt look of green, brown, and white.

People began coming to Granny Bent as soon as the roads and trails were passable to get chokecherry root and bark for cramps and boils, goldenseal for eyes made sore by smoky cabins, and other herbs for winter ailments. To Charley's disappointment, they brought no news of the war.

One February afternoon, Granny Bent took Charley with her to visit a farm on the other side of the mountain. She told him a woman there was expecting a baby soon and doing poorly, so she wanted to take her some yarbs that would give her strength for the birth. Glad to be away from the farm where he'd been weather-bound for so long, Charley enjoyed his tramp through the laurels and onto a road he'd never seen before. He hoped they would pass Sarie Giffen's farm, which he knew was somewhere in this direction, but they didn't. It was only when they headed back for home that he asked Granny Bent where it was, trying to sound casual as he did.

From atop Canaan, the old woman pointed to a trickle of smoke rising over tall evergreens a distance away. There was no cabin to be seen, only the smoke. "That's the Giffen place." She turned to grin at Charley, but she didn't add to what she'd already told him about pretty Sarie.

They traveled together, moving carefully along the narrow path bordered on each side by ravines. Charley wandered from one side of the road to the other to look down. On the right side, a path left the road and wound down to the bottom of the ravine where he saw creek water flowing swiftly. Over the yellow water stretched a plank bridge.

Charley said, "I can see a bridge down there. Where does it go?"

"To my side a the mountain. It's a shortcut, but I don' use it. If Canaan was a young mule and could climb good, I mighta. Mebbe we'll take it sometime later in the year when it's drier."

The last day of the month, the mountaineer whose wife was expecting her baby came riding up to the Bent cabin in the late-afternoon dusk. Jacob Hodder waved his lantern, cried out "Hello," and dismounted. Once inside the cabin, he took off his wide hat and shook drops of rain onto the dirt floor.

"Granny, it's truly comin' down out there now. It could be billy-hell to pay if it keeps up, but my Ellen's sayin' for ya to come now. Take yer pistol with ya for when ya come back. There's deserters hereabouts who'd rob ya. They jest come up here a little while back. They ain't fam'ly to no mountain folks."

Granny Jershua said, "I'm comin' with ya now, Jacob, and I'll take the pistol."

Charley watched her pull on heavy men's shoes, shove the pistol into her belt, then put on her old coat and hat. Next she lit her own lantern and threw a yellow oilcloth over her shoulders. Finally, she reached for her birthin' bag. At the door, she turned to Charley to say, "Don' open the door to nobody, ya hear? Lock and bolt up at night. I'll leave my sign on the porch that I ain't to home. Canaan and I'll be back soon as we can."

Charley nodded. He knew what she meant by her sign: a white rag tied to a porch post. He wished he could ask how long she expected to be away but couldn't in the presence of Hodder. Besides, hadn't she said once that babies came when they felt like coming and not before?

That night, it rained heavily—coming down in buckets, as they would say in New York. It kept up all night and for a good part of the next day. Though Charley ate only cold corn bread himself, he scrupulously fed the chickens and Malindy. He was lonely. The goose, though friendly now, was little company, and the chickens none at all. He went to his loft at dusk, wishing the old woman had a hound—or even better, a cat to take to bed with him. Noreen had had a pretty, soft, orange cat named Marmalade until Mr. Demarest said he didn't like cats and she gave it away to please him. He wished Marmalade was with him now.

After saying his prayers and a decade of the rosary, Charley fell asleep. He didn't sleep long. A wild honking from Malindy awakened him. Then came a fearful yowling from directly above him. It wasn't just screeching now but something more—scratching on the shingles right over him. The painter was back again—and hungry! Did she know he was here *alone*?

Too close to the mountain lion for comfort, Charley hurried down the ladder to the floor of the cabin. Standing on a chair, he got the long rifle from over the mantel and carried it over to the black window, which rattled with hail. Except for going to the fire to replenish it with wood, Charley Quinn didn't take his eyes from the window all night long.

Dawn found him still gripping the rifle, waiting for the great cat that had screamed all night to go away. What would happen if Granny came home while she was still there? Would she attack her or Canaan?

He waited till mid-morning and some hours of quiet. Then he cautiously stuck his head out first the back, then the front door. No painter—nothing but puddles of rainwater everywhere. Charley circled gingerly around the cabin to the shed and, with the rifle ready, pushed open the door. It was empty. He went next to the henhouse and there received a shock. The new boards he'd put up had been caved in entirely, and there was now a large hole. And he thought he'd done such good work! The boy held his breath as he lifted the latch and went in. Horror caught at him at what he saw. Blood, feathers, half-devoured hens everywhere—all were dead but three that huddled together on a roost at the very top of the coop. Why hadn't he heard the terrified chickens? He thought he knew. The racket Malindy had made and the screaming of the critter had drowned out the clamor the poor fowls made. Where was Malindy now? Had the painter got her, too?

He left the henhouse and looked around the farm. All at once, he saw the goose high atop an apple tree. She was safe. He ran to her, coaxed her down, and fed her kernels of corn by hand. Tonight, he vowed, she would stay in the cabin with him. So would the remaining hens.

Charley kept company with the chickens and the goose all that long, rainy day. Time after time, he went to the window hoping to see Granny Bent and Canaan coming up to the cabin, but he never did. What was keeping her?

Night fell, and with it came the knowledge that something must have happened. She would have sent somebody to him by now if she had had to stay away this long. The Hodders knew he was here.

That night, Charley Quinn slept on Granny's bed with the old rifle beside him as a bedfellow. Though weary, he tried to stay awake. Finally he dozed off, only to be startled awake by Malindy walking on him, flapping her wings, hissing and honking. The painter? It had to be. She was back if the goose was behaving like this. Where was she, though?

The boy listened hard. There was no caterwauling now, only a faint sound from the roof overhead. Scratching again? The painter was up there, trying to scratch away the shingles and leap down into the cabin from above. Well, she couldn't get through the roof, and in the morning she'd leave. He'd wait her out.

Then he'd leave, too. He'd made up his mind before he went to bed. If Granny Bent wasn't home by daybreak, he was going out after her. He'd leave Malindy and the hens inside and go out with the long rifle to find her. Right now, though, he'd try to get some sleep.

Finally, the scratching stopped entirely, and Malindy calmed down enough to go to sleep with her head under her wing. Charley slept, too, with the chickens roosting at the foot of the bed.

He awoke at eight-thirty by Johnny's watch, put some stale corn bread in his pockets, put on his shoes and the jacket Granny had given him, picked up the long rifle, and stepped out onto the front porch.

A sudden noise made him lean over the side of the

porch and look up. What he saw brought a gasp of terror from him. There, on the crest of the steep roof, stood the painter, staring down at him. As she crept slowly down the slope of the roof, her eyes were a pale yellow fire.

The critter had waited—kept quiet and waited all night long, waited for him to come out. Now she crouched down, her whiskers motionless as she tensed herself to spring.

Spring on him! Kill him! *No!*

Charley cried out wordlessly and flung himself off the porch, running down onto the soggy ground before the cabin. Instantly, he whirled around to face the painter.

In one fluid, arching motion, the mountain lion leapt off the roof and landed only a few yards from Charley. Here she stood, staring, twitching her tail. Then she gathered herself into a crouch again, readying herself to spring at him once more.

As she lifted herself off the ground, Charley brought the long rifle to his shoulder. He aimed and fired just as the spring toward him began and the painter's tawny chest was exposed to him between her massive paws.

Boy and great cat crashed down together onto the muddy earth—Charley from the recoil of the old piece and the critter from the bullet the long rifle had sent into her chest. The painter's huge head was only inches from his left hand, her beautiful golden body, huge, fearfully taloned feet, and long tail lying without movement.

He'd killed the critter! He'd shot and killed her all alone. He'd avenged his and Granny Bent's hens. A great shout of joy came from his throat. Who would dare call him a coward now? The big cat would have harmed him and the animals, and he'd gotten rid of her—all by himself, Charley Quinn had!

Charley didn't revel in his glory for long. He had something more important to do now—find Granny Bent. First, he'd reload the old rifle, then he'd go to the Hodder farm and look for her.

He found the going harder than before. Not only was the heavy rifle awkward, but the trails and road were still wet, slippery, and muddy. He came to the Hodder place at noon, later than he'd anticipated. As he'd walked, he had rehearsed what he was going to do and say. He'd talk as little as he could and would try his best to mimic mountain speech. By now, he'd heard enough of it to try an imitation.

He helloed the cabin, and when an old man came out, Charley called to him, "Where'd Granny Bent be?"

The old man came slowly up to him. "Ya want Jake? My boy went down to Hearne Hollow this mornin'. Ain't that what ya come for?"

Charley shouted, "No! Where'd Granny Bent be?"

"Her? She went back where she comes from." The old man pulled at his gray beard. "Two days back it was, she went. Say, ain'tcha her boy?"

Two days? Two days and she hadn't come home? Not even asking if she'd fetched a boy or a girl into the world, Charley backed away from the deaf old man, turned around, and headed at a run for the road. There was only one thing to do—walk along the narrow ridge road at the top of the ravines, calling and looking for her. For some reason, he felt no deserters or bandits had gotten her. She'd outtalk them all—and cure what ailed them, to boot.

For more than an hour, Charley scouted the narrow path, peering down thirty-foot ravines on either side. His calls—"Granny Bent, Granny Bent"—went unanswered.

And then, when he was just about to go back to her place, hoping she'd gotten there ahead of him, he saw the gleam of something bright yellow deep in a ravine to his right. Yes, that night she had put yellow oilcloth over her coat. Could she be down there?

He called her name but could hear nothing but the rushing of water in the stream below. He had to go down there and see for himself. Placing the long rifle in a hollow tree trunk at the edge of the road, Charley began to descend into the ravine, grabbing hold of thorny bushes, digging in with his heels, slipping and sliding until he finally reached the rocks that fringed the stream.

Yes, there she was, lying in a huddle on the farther bank of the creek. He could see by the wet marks on its banks that it had recently flooded. Charley recognized the spot. He'd seen it just days before. There had been a bridge here then, but now it was only planks lying scattered on exposed rocks in the still-rushing water.

"Granny!" shouted Charley.

A weak cry answered him. It was followed at once by a hoarse, grating, hawing noise. Canaan! That was a mule if he'd ever heard one. Where was he? Charley looked to his left. There, coming forward from an overhang of rock, was the black mule, still saddled and bridled. Canaan walked up to him, delicately picking his way over the rocks on Charley's side of the swollen creek.

The boy guessed what had happened. Canaan, carrying the old woman, had fallen off the road above.

Somehow they had slid together to the bottom of the ravine and traveled along it to this place where she would have expected a bridge to be. She found there was none, but all the same, she'd tried to ford the creek and been washed off Canaan's back into the water. Somehow she'd crawled to where she was on the opposite bank and Canaan had come back here. He'd stayed across the water from her.

What was Charley to do? Go across to Granny Bent and try to carry her back to the farm? No, he could never do that—not even drag her. She was bigger than he was and far heavier. Without Canaan, he could never get her back there, even by following the trail he could see on the other side of the ravine, which led to Granny's side of the mountain. How badly hurt was she? Cupping his hands to his mouth, he called over the noise of the stream, "Can you ride if I get him over, Granny?"

He saw her raise herself up on one elbow. He could barely hear her weak response. "Canaan won't cross the water."

16 THE TIDE AND THE RECKONING

Charley looked at the big mule. Oh, yes, Canaan would! he told himself. He went to the animal, grabbed the reins, and heaved himself into the saddle. Though the boy clucked to him and nudged him with his heels, Canaan refused to move an inch. How, then, to get him across? Charley thought hard. After a long moment, a memory came to him of an artilleryman he'd seen in Culpeper dealing with a horse that wouldn't pull a wagon. He had blindfolded the animal and hauled him along by force until he'd gotten the idea. Charley dismounted, whipped off his coat, and tied it over Canaan's eyes.

"Come on, you mule," he told the animal. "We can't let her stay here, and there isn't anybody at the Hodders who can help her now."

Slowly, Canaan came forward until his hooves touched the icy water. Then he reared, pawing the air above Charley's head with his big, iron-shod hooves. The boy barely dodged them as they came crashing down.

Gritting his teeth, Charley pulled on Canaan's bridle again, shouting, "Come on, you critter! We got to get wet!"

This time he managed to get the big mule down in the stream to his fetlocks and to Charley's waist. There Canaan stopped. The thrust of the bitterly cold current was powerful. Without Canaan between him and the main force of the swollen creek, Charley knew he'd be swept off his feet.

Shouting all the cuss words he'd learned at Culpeper camp and praying, too, Charley was able to pull the mule another five feet through the muddy water until it reached up to the animal's belly. Here the mule halted once more while Charley, who was in water to his shoulders now, had to grab at the horn of the saddle until he felt a submerged rock with his feet.

"Canaan, Canaan!" he yelled. "Keep going."

"Canaan, Canaan!" cried Jerusha Bent from the other bank, thirty feet away.

At her voice, the mule moved forward into deeper water and all at once was swimming. His quick movement made Charley lose his grip on the saddle horn and go under the torrent for a moment. Then he came up spluttering as the mule went past him swimming slantwise, carried along by the current. Canaan's long black tail floated in the water behind him, drifting in the boy's direction. Charley caught hold of it and held tight for his life, fearing the jagged rocks that stuck up in the bubbling water.

"Canaan, Canaan!" came the old woman's voice as the still-blindfolded mule struggled in the creek.

And then, kicking powerfully, Canaan swam into quieter water on the other side. He came up dripping onto the bank, fifty feet or so from where Granny Bent lay.

The moment he felt the bottom under his own feet, Charley let go of the animal's tail and waded up out of the water.

The first thing he did was take the blindfold off Canaan's eyes and lead him up to his mistress. Then he knelt down beside her to ask, "Are you hurt bad? I went to the Hodders. Then I came looking for you. How long have you been here?"

Her face was pale and her eyes sunken. "I hurt my leg. I been here two days and nights. I fell off Canaan and got over here, but he went back."

"Can you ride him, Granny?"

"I don' know, Charley. I'll have to be tied on."

He nodded grimly. He reached into his pocket and found his knife. Then he felt for Johnny's watch. It was there, too, but it had gotten wet. It would never run again. Well, he'd have it as a keepsake forever, anyhow. He told Jerusha Bent, "I'll cut the reins and tie you on with 'em. I can lead Canaan by the bridle if you tell me the way to get home on this trail. Can you get up?"

"I'll try to."

After slicing the rein from the bridle and then cutting it into two pieces, Charley boosted the old woman to her feet. He saw that she favored one leg. He led her to a moss-covered boulder and aided her to mount it. Then he brought Canaan up to her and hoisted her into the saddle. With one piece of rein, he tied her feet together under the mule's belly and with the other fastened her wrists to the horn.

"Hang on tight," Charley told her as he led the mule forward.

Granny Bent gave the directions in such a weak voice that Charley could scarcely hear which way to lead the mule. Sometimes he thought they must be lost as they threaded their way through laurel and trees, but in an hour's time, they came out on a slope from which he could see her farm. Canaan, not as weak as his mistress, began to move faster now, scenting familiar pastures. Charley ran beside him with one hand on Granny Bent's knee to steady her. When they came to the cabin door, Canaan halted of his own accord.

"I lost my pistol in the creek," said the old woman dreamily with closed eyes. When she opened them, her gaze lowered to the mountain lion stretched in tawny death before her porch. "*Charley!*" she exclaimed in wonder.

"I shot her. I had to."

"Ya shot the painter?"

"Yes, ma'am, with the old long rifle. She came two nights in a row and killed most of your hens and the rooster. I saved three of them and Malindy. They're inside. The critter jumped me this morning, so I had to shoot her."

For a long moment, old Jerusha stared over Charley's head, then a big smile creased her pale face. Shaking her head, she laughed and said, "Well, ain't ya the one, though? All in one day, ya shoot a ornery critter like this one and ya save a old woman's life! Ain'tcha the beatenist, bravest one, Mr. Skedaddle!"

"It's Quinn, Granny. Charles Stephen Quinn, that's my real name." He turned scarlet at her praise. "Let's get you down off Canaan and inside the house."

"Jest as ya say, Mr. Quinn. Git me to bed and cover me up so's I'll git warm. And after ya change into some dry clothes and see to the goose and hens, come out here and skin this critter and stretch her hide on the shed wall. I want folks to see her and know who done it. I'll mend fast once I get some yarbs inside me."

When Charley got her inside the cabin and into bed with three quilts over her, he built up the fire and shooed Malindy and the chickens out to fend for themselves for a time. Now Granny Bent was his chief duty. Without asking her for orders, he boiled water for sassafras tea, then fed it to her spoonful by spoonful. After that, he brought her corn bread, which he crumbled for her in water. He had eggs in a basket in the lean-to he could boil for supper.

Once she'd finished eating, Jerusha told him, "Skin that critter before sundown, Charley. Jest cut her up the middle and along the legs. Ya don' need the head. Bury that."

"Yes, ma'am, I will." Now he told her about going to the Hodder place and hearing she'd left. "I took the rifle with me when I left here to hunt for you. I couldn't get down the ravine where you were carrying it, so I hid it in a hollow tree that was there. Do you want me to go after it first?"

Her hand grasping his arm, she said, "Git it back here tomorrer when ya go tell the Hodders I been found. They got a baby girl there now."

"Granny, Jacob Hodder wasn't there. He was at the Hollow. I talked to his pa, I think. When Jacob finds out, he might come here."

"He will. Jacob will. So ya talked to his pa?"

"Yes, I tried to talk like you do."

"That was right bright of ya." And with those words, her eyes closed, and suddenly she fell asleep.

Now Charley went outside to take the bridle and saddle off Canaan and lead him to the shed to his fodder. After that, he went to look at the panther. In spite of Granny's instructions, he had no idea how to start skinning her.

As he stood there staring at the dead animal, he saw Jacob Hodder, trailed by a blue-tick hound, riding on a mule toward the cabin. Charley stood up and waited for the man.

As he dismounted, Hodder asked, "Where's Granny Bent? I see her rag still up on the porch."

Charley jerked his thumb toward the cabin. "I fetched her home. She's still sleepin'. She fell off her mule. Nothin's busted. She's jest tuckered out." Charley held his breath. What would Hodder think of his mountain talk?

The man only nodded. "That's what I reckoned. She musta fell somewheres. When I got back to my place, Pa told me a yer comin'. I tracked ya to the crick by the old bridge. I found her pistol by the bank and I'm fetchin' it back to ya." He opened his coat, took the pistol from his belt, and handed it to the boy.

Now he stared at the dead mountain lion as he scratched his chin. He went over to the huge cat, looked at her head and paws, then said slowly, "For certain this is Old Wry-foot. Granny musta been pert enough to shoot this

167

critter with Isaac's pa's old rifle when she got home."

"No, I done that before I come to yer place."

"Ya did?" The man's heavy brows rose in surprise.

"Yes, sir, she jumped me. I had the old rifle and I shot her. I'm goin' to skin her. Granny says to." Charley seized his opportunity for help now. "I never done that to anythin' so big as this. Jest to squirrels and rabbits."

The man laughed and said, "I reckon I ought to help ya, then."

"I'd be obliged to ya." Charley grinned at the mountaineer. Hodder hadn't praised him for his courage, but he could see the respect in his eyes.

Kneeling together, the boy and the man skinned the panther, buried the carcass, as it was unfit to eat, and stretched the rank-smelling golden hide with nails to the wall of the shed. Near sunset, Hodder left to go back home, but not before telling Charley news he longed to hear.

That morning, Hodder had talked with the first man to reach Hearne Hollow since winter began. He found out that the Johnny Rebs had been whipped twice in Tennessee and that Abe Lincoln had been elected president for the second time. A Yankee general by the name of Sherman had taken Atlanta and then gone eastward, across the state of Georgia and all the way to the ocean. Now he was marching north through the Carolinas to come up behind General Lee, who was still bottled up in Petersburg and Richmond. With bluebelly Yankees north of him and rising fast toward him from the south, General Lee was in trouble.

Charley's heart swelled with joy at what the mountaineer told him, though he kept his face expressionless throughout the telling.

When Hodder was out of sight, Charley took the white rag off the porch post and went back inside the cabin to see how Granny Bent fared. He found her lying quietly but with her eyes open. As he pulled a chair up to her bed, she asked, "Wasn' that Jake Hodder out there with ya?"

"Yes, he helped me skin the painter. He also told me what's going on in the war."

"What'd that be, Charley, that the South is losin'?"

"That's right, Granny," he replied, and he told her every word Hodder had spoken.

When he had finished, she only nodded and did not smile. She sighed as she told him, "I don' take no pleasure in all this warrin', though I want to see the North win out. Good men are dyin' on both sides. It's fool's work. I told ya before—some men dote on it 'cause it makes 'em feel brave. And they got to have other willies aroun' 'em when they do their killin', to see it and give 'em praise for doin' it. Ya mighta been right to skedaddle before ya did killin', little as ya are."

Jolted by these last words, Charley leaned forward, lowered his head, and put it on his arms, which were folded on his knees. He said thickly, "I skedaddled like you say, but before I did, I picked up a musket and shot and killed a Reb."

"Ya did?"

"Yes, I shot him, and he fell backward and then I ran. All the time, I keep seeing his face and my friends' faces, too. One of them was killed. The other one I hope was only wounded, but I'll never know for sure."

"Oh, Charley, that was a bad time for ya, and ya never talked about it before. Tell me about shootin' the Confed'rate now."

"He had a brown beard. I shot him in the shoulder, and he fell down."

"In the *shoulder*. Not in the chest or head?"

"That's right. I saw the blood."

Jerusha's old, wrinkled hand came up to pat his head. "Ya didn' kill him, Charley, not if he got hit where ya say ya shot him."

"I didn't?" Charley lifted his head, relief flooding his mind. "But I did run away, and that was a bad thing. It shows I'm a coward."

"Maybe you was then. But nobody'd dare call ya a coward after the brave things ya done today. Ya killed the critter and ya saved me with nary a soul to see what ya did, and that's what makes 'em deeds even braver. Ya got the grit to make yer way in the world jest fine. Ya could leave here tomorrer and go over the hills to the west if ya have a mind to."

So soon? Leave now? The thought had not occurred to Charley. Yes, he supposed he could. Granny Bent was sick and couldn't keep him here now if he wanted to go. Thanks to his good ear for music and speech, he could mimic mountain talk well enough to get through the hills by pretending to be a native of these parts. He knew the road westward at Hearne Hollow that would get him out of the Blue Ridge country. He pondered, looking about the cabin. Then he stared into the old woman's calm, dark eyes. There was no command in them that tried to hold him against his will. Nor was there a plea for him to stay because of her feebleness. That wouldn't be her way!

He made up his mind. "If it's all the same to you, I'd like to stay for a while longer."

"And I'd be honored to have ya under my roof, Charley Stephen Quinn."

Charley smiled. No, he couldn't leave her now. Mountain folks would come to help her out, but he didn't want that. He'd tend to her himself. That'd be the right thing to do, the thing the man of a family ought to do. She'd sort of turned into his family, his grandma. He'd never had a grandma up in New York because the old folks in his family were still in Ireland. And now he had a granny here, a mountain one!

17 HEADING OUT AGAIN

By the end of March, Jerusha Bent was well enough from her days of exposure to move around her cabin, cook for the two of them, and boil her own healing yarb teas. Once the word of her accident spread, mountain people came by, bringing her and Charley fresh-killed game, venison, and wild turkeys so they wouldn't go hungry.

No mountaineer praised Charley for his devotion to her—though he often heard her tell them, "Nobody can hold a candle to my boy here for pure goodness. He takes good care a me. Now go look at the hide a the critter on the shed wall. He killed her all alone with my old rifle that's near as tall as he is. There never was a painter the size a this one that I ever set eyes on before." And the visitors would go to the shed, look at the pelt, and return with nods of approval for Charley.

If they came back to the cabin, Granny Jerusha would sometimes add, lying for Charley's sake, so the story would spread, "My yarbs, they done good things for Charley here, but it took some time like all good doctorin' does. One yarb cleared the wool outa his head and another one got his tongue to workin'. My Charley's smart as any one of us." Sometimes then she'd ruffle Charley's hair and smile at him.

Occasionally, too, she'd go on to say to an audience of mountain folk, "I bet ya wonder where my boy came from but was too polite to ask. It'd only be natcheral for ya to wonder. After all, ya never seen him before I started fetchin' him to Hearne Hollow with me."

Oh, but old Jerusha was a skillful liar! Having said that, she'd go on to add without batting an eyelash, "He's a orphan from Kentucky. He come here last spring huntin' for some of his ma's kinfolks, who all went away to God knows where. Ya know how many fallin'-down cabins there is up here that folks left years ago and critters move into. Being the way Charley was when he got here, not talkin' good, he couldn' come up to ya and ask where they went or to ask ya for food and a roof over his head. His poor stummick got so empty, he tried to rob eggs outa my henhouse and I caught him doin' it. Because I could see there wasn' no harm in him and he was wool-headed to boot, I took him on. I'm mighty glad I did, seein' as how he came to hisself, thanks to my yarbs, and saved my life and saved the rest of us from that painter-critter that used to bedevil us. The way I see it, we all owe a debt to Charley for doin' us that service."

When she finished, the mountaineers would make sounds that let a proud Charley know that they did appreciate his killing the mountain lion that had come to other henhouses before coming to Granny Bent's.

Cois MacRae came one day to get rheumatism yarbs

for his granny. The mountain boy was ill at ease. He went with Charley to examine the golden pelt, then for quite a while he stood silently beside him while Charley waited for him to speak.

Finally, Cois opened up and said, "I heard tell ya shot Old Wry-foot with that old long rifle Granny Jerusha keeps."

"That's what I did."

"Did the piece kick like a mule?"

"Kicks worse'n Canaan. It knocks me on my back ever' time I fire it."

"I don' think I'd want to fire it."

Charley said modestly, enjoying this, "I don' take no pleasure in it." Now he added, "I ain't no Bent by blood, no kin at all to Granny here. How come ya jumped me down in Hearne Hollow, Cois?"

Cois shook his yellow head. "Because the fust time I saw ya, ya were in her comp'ny. I figgered ya for a far-out relative a the Bents, and us MacRaes is supposed to fight Bents whenever we sees 'em."

"Well, I ain't no Bent, so there ain't no cause to fight me anymore—long as ya don' give Sarie Giffen no more trouble." Charley put his thumbs into the suspenders old Jerusha had woven to hold up the new homespun pants she'd sewed for him. He was shooting up fast now, and someday he'd be as tall as Johnny had been when he went off to war.

Cois, now shorter than Charley, looked at the thumbs, then shook his head. "I don' mean no harm to Sarie. I like to josh her to see her face turn red."

"Well, don' ya do that anymore. Josh some other girls

that might take to it better—and turn redder. But, on second thought, I don' think ya ought to say anythin' at all that shames any girl to hear. They can't fight ya back. It ain't manly to do what you did."

Charley watched the other boy swallow and look away. Cois's hand stroked the mountain lion's hide, ruffling the stiff, tawny fur. He asked, "Where'd ya learn to shoot, Charley?"

"Where I come from. My big brother, Johnny, he saw to it I learned."

"Where's he now?"

"Dead. Killed at Gettysburg."

Cois nodded. "My cousin, he died there, too. We miss him."

Cois MacRae turned now and walked away, leaving Charley thinking sadly of Johnny and of the war still going on here in Virginia.

Some of the Giffen family came one day very late in March, Sarie with them. They visited with Granny and admired the pelt. While the older Giffens were inside the cabin with Granny, Charley and Sarie struck out walking together through the still, bare-limbed apple trees.

Because the shy girl was silent, Charley started the conversation. He cleared his throat and said, "Cois MacRae won' bother ya no more, Sarie."

"How come he won't?" Sarie glanced at him from under shining black lashes.

" 'Cause I talked to him about ya and told him not to say things to ya that ya don' want to hear." How easily the mountain speech came to him by now.

175

Sarie smiled. "Thank ya, Charley. Are ya my knight in shining armor?"

"What'd that be?" Charley was taken aback.

"The old-time horseback rider that saves ladies who're in a fix."

"Where'd you hear about that, Sarie?"

"In a book I'm readin' now. I don' make it out so good yet, 'cause I ain't far past the ABC's, but it has pitchers in it. The last preacher who came through told me about one of the pitchers. It had a knight in armor, and armor allus shines real bright, 'cause it's made out of pure silver. There was a lady in the pitcher, too. The preacher said that the knight had saved her from bein' ate up by a dragon that snorted fire. The knight's holdin' her so tenderly to his armor." Sarie Giffen sighed.

A knight? Charley marveled. Was that how she saw him, somebody who used to be a Bowery Boy? It was better being thought a knight. His chest swelled as he basked under her admiring gaze.

"How come you think that about me, Sarie? I ain't so much." He felt the heat rise in his cheeks as his eyes fell from hers.

" 'Cause ya fought for me and killed the painter and saved Granny Bent's life. Ain't that enough to be a knight?"

"Oh, I dunno, Sarie." Charley fell silent, not knowing what else to do.

Just then a woman's high-pitched cry called, "Sarie, time to go now! Come on to the cabin."

The girl left Charley, running easily under the trees and into the cabin to say goodbye to Granny. Charley followed slowly after, hating to see the Giffens go. Maybe he ought to help the womenfolks up onto their mules. That'd be courteous, the sort of thing a knight should do.

But before he could reach them, Sarie came flying up to him over the spring grass. She pulled something out of her pocket and pressed it into his hand. It was a lock of her black, silken hair tied with a piece of frayed rose-colored ribbon. Grinning, Charley put it inside his shirt while she watched, smiling, too. Then she ran back to her mule and scrambled up onto it by herself.

On the fourth of April by Charley's homemade calendar, Jacob Hodder came once more to the Bent farm. He'd been to Hearne Hollow that morning and heard there that General Lee and his army had marched out of Petersburg and Richmond, leaving these cities to the Yankees. A peddler from the East who had brought the news had said everybody figured Lee's soldiers would go ahead of the Yankees and take refuge in the mountains to go on fighting from here.

As Charley and Granny Bent stood together on their porch listening, Jacob Hodder told them, "That'll mean fightin' around these parts and plenty a trouble for us. Fightin' up here could go on for years and mebbe never come to a end. It won' be like battles on bluegrass country flatland that are over till the next one starts. Up here it'll be goin' on all the time with our boys and Yankee soldiers hidin' out and huntin' one another and comin' to take away our animals and what we grow and need for ourselves."

Shaking his head, the mountaineer rode off to take his war news to other farms.

The minute he was out of sight through the trees,

Granny Bent grabbed Charley by the arm. "Yer goin' to go west tomorrer mornin', Charley! Hodder's dead right. The Confed'rates will come up here. It'll be the only place they can go to now. Ya mebbe won' be able to fool 'em that yer a Kentucky boy like ya can Hodder and the others. They'll be men from Kentucky among 'em. They could ask questions of ya and mebbe wind up with the truth. That'd make 'em mad as hornets and they'll shoot ya. And even if they don' think ya to be a Yankee, they'll make ya go into their army. They could be gettin' short a men by now. Yer gettin' tall. Folks hereabouts'll tell how ya killed the painter, so they'll find out ya shoot good. That could make 'em come here and take ya away with 'em right off. Either way, bein' shot as a Yankee or shoved into their army, it'd be terrible bad for ya. Ya have to leave before they git here. There ain't time for ya to lay back and ponder goin'."

Shaken, Charley sat down on the porch beside the rocker she had just sat in. He hadn't expected to go—and so suddenly. He hadn't thought of where the Johnny Rebs would go if they knew they were losing. Of course, they'd come up here! The mountains were their natural place of refuge, their last hope to keep the war going. Lee's men would be welcome here among other Confederates, and they could hide and fight out of here for years, as Hodder had said.

"I guess I do have to go," the boy said sadly. All at once, he thought of something else. He turned to Granny Bent to ask worriedly, "What about you? Does anybody up here know you used to be in the Underground Railroad? If the soldiers find out, they'll come here after you."

"Don' ya fret over that. Nobody here who's still alive knows what me and Isaac did. Them that fetched us the black folks were older'n us, and so were the folks we fetched the blacks to. They're all dead now."

Charley let out a sigh of relief. At least Granny Bent would be all right.

She went on quickly, "I'll fix ya corn bread and bacon and boiled eggs in a cloth to take with ya. There's water lots of places, so ya won't thirst."

Charley said, "I'll chop plenty of wood for you before I go." This time he let out a sigh of regret. "But I won't be here to plant your corn, Granny."

"Don' fret over me, I tell ya. I can take care a myself, but bless ya for thinkin' of me." She reached out to run a gnarled old finger down his freckled cheek. "Somebody'll come to plant my corn."

"Sarie Giffen?"

"Is there another Sarie, Charley?"

"No, ma'am." Charley touched the black hair coiled inside his shirt. That would leave with him as his and Sarie's secret.

The old woman asked, "Will ya write me when ya get to the west and are settled somewheres?"

"But you can't read!"

"Sarie's learnin'. I reckon she'll come over to live with me soon. She wants to be a yarb woman someday. The Giffens can spare her, and she hankers to start learnin' from me. There'll be a place for her when ya go. I'll keep her safe. Write to the storekeeper in Hearne Hollow. He'll see to it the letters git to me."

"Sure, I'll write. I'll write my sister in New York, too, when I'm settled someplace. Maybe Sarie'll practice writing by answering me?"

Old Jerusha gave him a fleet, knowing look and then asked softly, "Mebbe ya'll think on comin' back to visit her and me once the war's over and done with?"

Come back here? Charley turned to gaze at the great green hills that had sheltered him for the strangest, yet most satisfying, months of his life. It had been a dangerous refuge, but he had truly proven himself up here—not as a Bowery Boy in the Bowery, nor as a soldier in the Wilderness, but high in these mountains. He'd done it alone, with nobody urging him on or praising him for his courage. And it was more pure for having been done alone.

Charley Quinn drew himself up to his full height, looked Granny Bent full in the eyes, and said, "I reckon when I get to be as tall as I'll ever be, I'll be back. This ain't so bad a place for a man to settle."

"No, it ain't," she agreed.

AUTHOR'S NOTES

Charley Quinn is a fictional boy. Yet his adventures during the climactic years of 1864–1865 could easily have taken place in real life. There were hundreds of drummer boys in the Union Army at that time. It cannot be presumed that all of them stayed constantly at their posts when it is established that at the Civil War's end there were 199,105 Yankee deserters (100,000 Confederates also "skedaddled").

In taking Charley, my Bowery Boy, to the war in early 1864, I have made use to some extent of Frank Wilkeson's published account of his own adventures. He was an adult New York artilleryman at the time—not a juvenile drummer boy—but he marched down Broadway to the Battery, endured a drunken, gambling voyage to Alexandria, Virginia, and from there went by guarded troop train to the huge Union Army camp at Culpeper. "Bounty jumping" was rife in the later years of the war. In 1864, New York enlistees were paid $477 each to join up. Guards did not let these men out of their sight, so they couldn't run off and reeniist for money somewhere else. Wilkeson was present as a participant at the Battle of the Wilderness, which is variously described by writers who were eyewitnesses. All agree as to its horror. Human bones and metal relics of the battle are still being found there. Grant lost 17,500 men here, and Lee close to 8,000.

My material regarding the 140th New York Veteran Volunteers is factual. They were at Gettysburg, and they were among the first hit by the powerful Confederate offensive at the Wilderness. After this battle, they fought again fifteen miles away at Spottsylvania four days later. In 1865, they saw the end of the war, besieging the Confederates outside Richmond, the southern capital. Present at the surrender at Appomattox, they were disbanded in 1865. An Irish-American unit from New York, they suffered heavier losses at the Wilderness than at Gettysburg. For finding material about them in the section of the book that takes place in New York, I thank my editor, Andrea Curley.

The Civil War, America's costliest war in terms of lives (Yankee dead, 359,528; Confederate dead, 258,000), ended with Robert E. Lee surrendering on April 9, 1865. He and his forces never did get to the Blue Ridge Mountains to carry on the war from there as guerrillas, though this was the plan some high-ranking Southern officers entertained. Had they done so, they would have found Confederate deserters there in numbers.

It would have been quite within the realm of possibility for Charley Quinn to get a close look at Generals Ulysses S. Grant and George Meade in Culpeper during April 1864. They were there. General Robert E. Lee, according to legend, actually attempted to lead a charge of a Texas unit in person at the Battle of the Wilderness. He was supposed to have been turned back by worried Texas troops to join fellow Confederate General James Longstreet to observe the action from afar.

I have written here of black freedmen working for the Yankees for wages in Virginia. They did work in a variety of jobs, receiving money for their labors for the first time in their lives. It is not unlikely that they found a New York Bowery accent strange and incomprehensible.

Two hundred thousand black men served in the Confederate Army as laborers and servants. In the Union Army, they were enlisted as soldiers. Though there were black soldiers in Virginia at the time of the Battle of the Wilderness, they were not yet pressed into service. Later, they fought at Petersburg and other places, and many distinguished themselves. Surely, as boys, some of these men had been moved north via the Underground Railroad, a group of slavery-hating people south and north who secretly moved fugitive slaves from southern states into northern ones where they would be free men and women. It actually functioned in the Virginia mountains. My Thad Porter's visit to Jerusha Bent not only would have been a very courageous thing to do, but also not improbable.

Unfortunately, the black soldiers were not accorded fair treatment by the government that had freed and enlisted them, supposedly to fight. They did a larger amount of ditch digging and breastwork construction than white soldiers, and not until the final year of the war were they paid as much as their white comrades-in-arms. The Civil War may have settled the political issue but not the racial one. It took another ninety years before legislative action was taken against racial discrimination.

The Bowery Boys is the name of a street gang made famous by a group of young actors in movies in the 1940s. This was a theatrical group only. In the 1850s and 1860s, there actually was a gang by that name in the rowdy Bowery section of New York City. And the Dead Rabbits were their true rivals. Their standard was a dead rabbit, which they carried on a pole as they went into street fights. They sported sewed-on red stripes on their trousers. The Bowery Boys wore a particular uniform also—black plug hat, black coat and trousers, red shirts, and high-heeled boots. These two gangs were not criminal gangs in the 1860s, but after the Civil War, they were replaced by new gangs of young criminals.

What I have written of 1864 New York is culled not only from books but from issues of *The New York Times* of the day. The places, Niblo's Theater, P. T. Barnum's, Genin's, Macy's, Tiffany's, were real New York institutions. The very successful Metropolitan Fair with its "hairy eagle" opened early in April that year. (I do not know what became of the "eagle" in later years.) Harlem and Queens were rural, and so was Brooklyn. Though there were no automobiles yet, the traffic congestion on Broadway was notorious. Probably surprising to most of today's New Yorkers, and to my astonishment, the city was actually considering subway transport during the Civil War to relieve the congestion on the aboveground streets. Later subways were built and today are of course an important feature of New York's public transportation system.

In writing of the Blue Ridge Mountains in Civil War times, I have kept as close as I could to what my sources tell me things were like then. As I have pointed out, deserters abounded. The laurel thickets and rock caves also sheltered bandits who pledged allegiance to neither side in the conflict. The hills were dangerous, indeed, in 1864. Charley's accent would mark him quickly as a non-Southern "outlander." If he wasn't shot out of hand, he could have been hanged as a spy. Actually, on both sides such things happened to boys as young as he was. These mountains were chiefly Confederate in sympathy. Men who'd enlisted in the Confederate Army for short terms came home to plant crops and sometimes stayed on. They could have recognized a Yankee deserter for what he was and would have put him in peril of his life.

For the eyes and ears of young readers who often find dialect difficult, I have toned down the speech of my mountaineers to an approximation of the way they very likely would have sounded in 1864. I have not used *tarnal* and *bodacious* and other words and expressions that would need defining, but have tried to keep the flavor without going into a broad hillbilly dialect that sounds too cartoon-strip. These people led hard lives and were worthy of respect. They embodied then (and still do) many of the proud, self-sufficient, frugal American-character concepts we still hold dear.

I have written here of a mountain lion attack on a human being. Such occurrences were never common, but they did happen. Within the last few years, there have been several attacks on children in wilderness areas. Animal behavior experts believe the encroachment of more and more people is the cause of this unfortunate behavior.

Virginia librarians aided me. In particular, I thank Ann Robson of the Culpeper Public Library for helping me with some questions. In writing *Charley Skedaddle*, I owe debts to many people. When it comes to maps, I must thank James Rothenberger and Jim Sanders. For material on drums and drumming, I am indebted to Jean Pierre Barricelli, George Carroll, Antony Ginter, Master Sergeant Ed Kiefer (Ret.), and Hazel Simon.

Margaret Davidson of Riverside, California, gave me the unpublished familial record of her England-born, New York-based drummer boy grandfather, Henry Hilton Davidson, who was actually at the battle of the Wilderness and served in the Union Army from 1862 to 1865, taking his drum home with him at its end. He was not my model for Charley, however. Mr. Davidson was seventeen—though undersized—when he joined up in 1862 and was picked as a drummer boy. Later he grew to a full six feet and much later became chaplain of the Union Army veterans group, the Grand Army of the Republic. Would that he had written his own account of the Wilderness for military historians!

Last of all to be thanked, and most of all because of his many efforts on my behalf in writing *Charley Skedaddle*, is my brother, Colonel Phillip W. Robbins, U.S.A. (Ret.). A student and aficionado of Civil War history, he aided me greatly with facts I, though a former librarian, would have been hard-pressed to find.

—Patricia Beatty
June 1986